KING OF NEW YORK 2

Lock Down Publications and Ca$h
Presents
KING OF NEW YORK 2
A Novel by *T.J. EDWARDS*

Lock Down Publications

P.O. Box 870494
Mesquite, Tx 75187

Visit our website @
www.lockdownpublications.com

Lock Down Publications
Like our page on Facebook: Lock Down Publications @
www.facebook.com/lockdownpublications.ldp
Cover design and layout by: **Dynasty Cover Me**
Book interior design by: **Shawn Walker**
Edited by: **Sunny Giovanni**

Stay Connected with Us!

Text **LOCKDOWN** to 22828 to stay up-to-date with new releases, sneak peaks, contests and more…
Or **CLICK HERE** to sign up.
Thank you.

Like our page on Facebook:

Lock Down Publications: Facebook

Join Lock Down Publications/The New Era Reading Group

Visit our website @
www.lockdownpublications.com

Follow us on Instagram:

Lock Down Publications: Instagram

Email Us: We want to hear from you!

Submission Guideline.

Submit the first three chapters of your completed manuscript to ldpsubmissions@gmail.com, subject line: Your book's title. The manuscript must be in a .doc file and sent as an attachment. Document should be in Times New Roman, double spaced and in size 12 font. Also, provide your synopsis and full contact information. If sending multiple submissions, they must each be in a separate email.

Have a story but no way to send it electronically? You can still submit to LDP/Ca$h Presents. Send in the first three chapters, written or typed, of your completed manuscript to:

LDP: Submissions Dept
Po Box 870494
Mesquite, Tx 75187

DO NOT send original manuscript. Must be a duplicate.

Provide your synopsis and a cover letter containing your full contact information.

Thanks for considering LDP and Ca$h Presents.

T.J. Edwards

Chapter 1
Tristian

Sweat poured down my back and slid down the side of my face. My stomach felt like it was in knots. My left eye twitched repeatedly. I bit into my bottom lip and kept my pistol aimed at my brother, Showbiz, looking for a clear shot to take him out of his misery. He had his arm wrapped around Perjah's neck with his .45 automatic pressed to the back of her head. The duct tape that he'd placed around her eyes had come half way off. She whimpered underneath him. We were in the basement of my brownstone. It felt like the heat had been turned all the way up.

My other brother, Miguel, was laid out on the basement floor full of slugs, courtesy of me. He shivered as blood leaked out of him and created a puddle that mixed with that of Perjah's niece. She lay sprawled out on her stomach, deceased.

Showbiz tightened his grip on Perjah and jerked her aggressively. "Drop that muthafucking gun, Tristian, or I'ma slump this bitch! Do it!" He hollered.

"Please don't let him kill me, Tristian. I ain't did nothing to him. Please." Perjah begged.

About three months ago, Perjah's brother, Flex, had murdered my brother Showbiz's son. In retaliation, not only had Showbiz got his revenge by murdering Flex, but he'd killed Flex's daughter and murdered a party full of people that were celebrating Flex's birthday. Now he had his sights on murdering Flex's sister, Perjah, and her daughter Brittany.

Brittany was laid on the floor sobbing. She was nine years old and paralyzed from the waist down. She'd been a victim of a shootout that myself and my brother had with Flex and his crew. Ever since that day I'd been a part of her and her mother's life trying to right the wrongs that my brother had caused. It wasn't known whether the bullet was from us or somebody else's gun. On the day the shooting happened, more than half of the shooters, including myself and my brother, were using .45s. The only thing I knew for sure was that I'd not been the one to have shot her because I was bussing in the opposite direction of her. In fact, when the shooting started I was the one that jumped on top of her to shield her from the attacks. In the process, I caught two slugs to my back. Thankfully none of them had pierced my spinal cord.

"Drop that muthafucka, Tristian! On my mother, I ain't gon' say that shit again, Kid!"

Brittany started to cough on the floor. She flipped onto her back and began to shake uncontrollably. It sounded like she was choking. Her eyes rolled into the back of her head. I don't know what came over me, but out of instinct, I dropped my guard and lowered my pistol. I kneeled beside her and got ready to take her within my arms when I heard the screeching of brakes. Seconds later, the shooting began in rapid fashion.

Doom. Doom. Doom. Bop. Bop. Bop. Over and over again. It sounded like a war movie with the volume of television turned the all the way up. The house was being rocked by the assault.

I grabbed Brittany into my arms. Her eyes continued to roll into the back of her head. I smacked her on the cheek. "Brittany, Brittany, baby, what's the matter?" I asked not knowing what to do.

I could hear the windows to my house shattering upstairs. The bullets continued to fly, slamming into the brownstone.

Perjah screamed as Showbiz flung her to the basement floor. He stood over her and pulled the trigger twice. *Boom. Boom.* She inhaled the bullets and laid on her back with her arms out stretched.

"Noooo!" I hollered, jumping up and running at him with my gun raised.

Before I could squeeze the trigger, he pulled his four times. *Boom. Boom. Boom. Boom.* His bullets slammed into my chest and stomach, knocking me backward. I dropped my gun and fell to the floor in intense pain. My vision was hazy. I smelled a strong stench of bile and piss. I watched Showbiz stand over Brittany. He aimed his gun and pulled the trigger twice. *Boom. Boom.* Ending her life. It was the last thing I saw before I passed out and everything faded to black

* * *

The next time I woke up, I saw that I was being pushed on a gurney. I had an oxygen mask on my face. There were what seemed like five nurses all around me, rushing me to the emergency room. There were IVs in my arm, and it felt like somebody had parked a truck on my chest. Every time I tried to inhale it felt like I was breathing in ice sickles. My eyes bugged out of my head. The pain was so incredible that all I could do was close my eyelids as I struggled to breathe on my own.

I didn't open my eyes again until fourteen hours later as I felt something being pushed into my veins. There was a nurse with a blue mask covering half her face. She looked into my eyes and smiled. There was a big needle in her hands. She flicked it with her fingernail and squirted some of the contents in the air before forcing my head to the side and jamming the needle into my neck with reckless abandon.

I flopped around on the bed as she dug it further and further into me until I was screaming at the top of my lungs. It was so painful that I passed out again.

When I came to, Perjah was standing at my side with her hand within my own. "Tristian. Tristian. Oh my God, baby, you okay?" She cried, rubbing the side of my face.

I jerked away from her and opened my eyes wide. I tried to swallow but there was a huge lump in my throat. It felt like a rock. Not only couldn't I swallow, but the sights of Perjah standing before me was enough to drive me out of my mind. *How could it be possible*, I wondered.

Perjah took a step back. "Nurse! Nurse! He's awake. Help! Something isn't right!" She hollered, running to the door.

The next thing I knew there was an Asian female nurse that ran into the room. She placed her hand on my forehead and checked the monitors that I was hooked up to. She was reading them and scrunched her eyebrows. "His blood pressure is incredibly high. We're going to have to bring that down. Ma'am, I'm sorry but I'm going to have to ask you to step out of the room." She waved Perjah off and tended to me.

Perjah shook her head. "I ain't leaving him again. I'm not going nowhere. I need to know what's the matter with him. Tell me what is going on," she demanded.

The nurse alerted the hospital staff. They led Perjah out of the room before they began to work on me. Once again, I passed out. It was simply too much for me to process.

* * *

I didn't wake up until a weeks later. This time when I did, not only was Perjah standing at my side, but I saw that my mother was sitting on the couch next to the window looking out of it. Her chin was resting in her hand, and she held a worried look in her brown eyes.

I smacked my lips together and began to cough harshly. "Damn."

Perjah rushed into action. She grabbed a juice from my night table and slammed a straw into it. "Here you go, baby. Drink some of this." She placed the straw to my lips.

I sucked out of it. The cold liquid seemed to soothe the fire in my lungs and throat. I drank it so fast that the carton wound up crinkling. Perjah grabbed another one and helped me to sip out of that one as well. The second one pushed me over the edge. I felt so much better. I closed my eyes for a second and tried to gain a hold of myself.

My mother rushed to my side, slightly nudging Perjah out of the way. "Baby, are you okay?" She asked, holding her hand on my forehead.

I swallowed and nodded. "Yeah, what happened to me?"

Since my mother was taking up one whole side. Perjah settled and walked around to my right side, so she could touch me as well. "Baby, your brother shot you as you were getting out of your car. I saw it. You don't remember any of it?" She asked with watery eyes.

"Them dirty muthafuckas just jealous of my son. He's the new king, and they hate that shit." My mother snapped.

I shook my head once again. "Nah, shorty. I don't. Which one of my brothers did this to me?"

She shrugged. "I don't know, baby. All I saw was you pull in front of the house. I was looking out of the window, waiting for you. I saw Showbiz's Benz truck roll up, then both the drivers' and the passengers' doors to his truck opened. Both occupants got out, ran up to your truck, and that's when the shooting started. I was so scared that I grabbed Brittany and pulled her to the floor. We didn't get up until his truck screeched away from the curb. Five minutes later, Shapiro rolled up and ordered me to not call the police or the ambulance. He said that he had it under control. I didn't know what else to do, so I let him handle everything. Right now you're at David's Mercy Hospital out in Brooklyn. This is a private quarter of the hospital, and I was told to contact Shapiro as soon as you came to." She kissed me on the cheek and rubbed my chest. "I'm so glad that you're okay though."

I winced and tried to sit up. I adjusted the pillow behind me before laying my head back on to it. I had a horrible migraine but at the same it felt like my body was floating on air. I figured it was the morphine they were pumping into my system.

My mother took a of my hand and interlocked our fingers. She kissed the back of it. "Son, you've been here for nearly a month. A lot has happened since you've been down, but none more important than your father. He's been hospitalized as well. He's incredibly sick. The doctors aren't giving him more than a few weeks. I'm sorry to be the one to break this news to you." She smiled weakly and kissed my cheek. "Hopefully they'll discharge you from this place before he passes on."

My father's image came into my mind. I couldn't imagine my life without him being a part of it. For as long as I could remember my father had always been there for me. He always pushed me to become the best possible version of myself. It was him that had approved for me the rights to his throne. The thought of him passing away was enough to make me sick on the stomach.

I exhaled loudly and looked up to my mother. "Mama, you know I gotta go at these niggas' heads for what they've done to me. I can't honor this. I might not know who pulled the trigger, but I know how Showbiz gets down. Ever since my Pops told him that I was next in line for the throne he's been coming at me from every angle. As soon as I'm strong enough I'ma put a stop to this once and for all." I meant that.

My brother, Showbiz, was a loose cannon. He was a low life scumbag that didn't give a fuck about taking a life. He was self-centered, egotistical, and a hot head who didn't like taking L's on no level. My Pops had said that whichever one of his sons could come up with fifteen million dollars in five months he'd place them on his throne and give them all of the power and political influence that came along with it. Around this time, we'd been months away from helping a senator to become the next mayor of New York City. The fifteen million would be used to help get Senator Jefferey Grant become elected. With him in office, my family, the Vegas, would have supreme control of the drug flow in and out of the city. We'd be able to bully the game and have judges and district attorneys at our feet.

My father was originally from Havana, Cuba. It was our homeland. Back home we'd recently obtained a hundred acres of sugarcane fields. Twenty-five percent of those acres had already been transformed into poppy plants to create heroin, and another twenty-five percent was coco leaves for the procession of cocaine. These acres were supposed to render onto our generational wealth and prestige. My brother was power-hungry. He felt that my father's throne was his birth right. He was my father's first born. He had me by three years.

My mother lowered her eyes. "Oh, we gon' get 'em, baby. But it has to be the right time. We can't afford a war within the family at this time. Your father is on his sick bed. On top of that, the Gomez family has waged war against all of Chico's children. That includes your sister, Brooklyn, as well. She's innocent in all of this."

Perjah rubbed my chest again. "Baby, they've already shot you twice in your chest. Luckily you didn't die. Why can't we just pick up and leave? There's no reason for all of this senseless violence. Both myself and Brittany need you. We can't have you if you're locked in somebody's prison or worst, yet dead."

My mother scoffed. "Well, I need him too. He is a king. Them rotten son of a bitches aren't going to get away with what they did to my son; you better believe that. For now, I'm imploring you to lay low son. There are millions of dollars at stake here with you behind the wheel. Your connections are about to go through the roof. Trust me when I tell you this. Senator Grant is in debt to this family. He is well aware of our demands, and he intends to fulfill his obligations as promised. An internal war could potentially be devastating for our standings in the social climate of New York. We have to avoid any and all detriments at this point, all the while laying in wait for the right time to strike. Until further notice you'll have a security detail that will insure you are well guarded at all times. These are men from my bloodline who are trained, heartless assassins that will kill at the drop of a hat for your mother, and now for you. If those rotten brothers of yours so much as cross the line any time soon then we'll be forced to abandon our show of patience and will murder them on sight."

There was a knock at the door. Shapiro, our family's lawyer and the right hand man, peeked inside the room. "Tristian, you're up. Do you feel strong enough to talk?" he asked stepping all the way into the room with two body guards following close behind him.

My mother walked around and grabbed Perjah's hand. "Come on, baby, let's go down to the cafeteria and catch a bite to eat. Let's allow these men to talk business. Besides, seeing as you care about my son so much, I think it's imperative that you and I get to know each other."

Before they left the room, Perjah rushed to my side and kissed my lips. "I'll see you in a minute, baby. I'm so glad that you're okay."

Shapiro ordered his guards to stand outside of the door, and make sure that nobody can come inside. After this, he closed the door and walked up to me. "Is this Showbiz's work?"

I shrugged my shoulders. "I can't say for certain. Perjah said she saw his truck pull behind me before two occupants got out and shot me. She didn't say whether it was Showbiz or Miguel. What makes you ask me this question?"

He pushed his glasses up on his nose. "Ever since you've been in the hospital your brother has been trying to convince your father that you're already dead. Your father is so sick that he's ready to hand him the throne. Showbiz has already been given the tour of Havana where the Vega's fields are. He's met with some of the workers and has been introduced to the top ranking kingpins in Cuba. They've been told that he'll oversee the operation after your father passes on." He ran his fingers through his hair and shook his head. "This is nuts."

I frowned and swallowed. I felt like everything was slipping through my fingers. I couldn't allow for Showbiz to become king of our family. He was too impulsive and all about himself. I gave it no more than five years and we'd all be either in prison or slain by another family. Either way it was a recipe for disaster. I had to get up out of that bed and reclaim what was given to me. "Well, as you see I'm still alive. I won't be in this bed long. My father has already crown me to run this family. You have to see to it that nothing changes."

Shapiro nodded. "I'll do all that I can. Your brother has already aligned himself with a bunch of street savages out of Harlem. They've fully taken over the Red Hook Houses in Brooklyn and he's already rocking and rolling. He'd used the fifteen million that he came up with to strengthen his regime. No matter if your father hands him over the throne or not, he's pretty strong so we'll have our work cut out for us."

I winced in severe pain as I struggled to sit all the way up in that bed. Sweat slid down the side of my face. It wasn't because I was hot, it was because I was in pain like never before. "Come here, Shapiro," I ordered looking him over.

He slowly made his way to the bed and stood about an arm's length away from me. "Sir?"

I grabbed him by the tie and pulled him until my forehead was only inches away from his. "Do you remember when we were in my father's office, right after Senator Grant had won the election, and my father told you that from that point on you were to treat me as if I was him? Do you?"

He slowly nodded his head. "Yes, sir, I do."

"Well, I am telling you to let my father know that I am alive and well. I will be fully functional and ready to lead in a matter of weeks. The throne is still

17

mine. I am ready to kill for it just as much as, Showbiz. If muthafuckas wanna test my gangsta and think its sweet because I've always been the respectful and cerebral child, then let's get it. I know what it takes to be a king. I just have to turn down the heat of my heart and get as grimy as the next nigga. Fix this shit and give me two weeks."

Shapiro stared into my light brown eyes with his green ones for a long time. Then he shook his head. "I've always seen more of your father in you than in either one of your siblings. I believe in you, Tristian. Your heart is pure. I swear to honor you just as I have always honored your father. I'll take care of things to the best of abilities. You focus on getting stronger. Your time table cannot exceed two weeks. There is far too much taking place. Your presence is needed more sooner than later."

I laid there in the bed for a long time with my eyes opened, just staring at the ceiling after he left. I was starting to understand that in order for me to become king I was going to have to become just as cold and as heartless as my brothers. They didn't fight fair. They did whatever it took to win and advance in the game. I had to be the same way. Even though I ultimately wanted to become more than just a drug lord, my legacy would start with sitting upon my father's throne.

Chapter 2

I was released from the hospital three days later. My mother had my brownstone emptied and moved to her gated community outside of Bayside. She'd already footed the bull and purchased me a five-bedroom, five-bathroom mini-mansion right off the river. When stepped into it, it was already fully furnished and designed how she felt I'd like it. To be honest, the interior of the place was the furthest thing from my mind. I had to focus on getting healthy, so I went right into beast mode. I had a universal gym placed into the basement portion of the mansion, along with a treadmill. I was dead-set on working out religiously, every single day until I got my strength and stamina back.

I had been wearing a vest during my attack, but two of the bullets had gon' into the same hole, forcing one of them to become lodged inside my chest. The second bullet that penetrated me slammed into the right side of my collarbone and broke it. Out of both injuries this was the one that hurt me the most. Anytime I moved my right arm it felt like somebody was trying to yank it out of socket. The pain was often times unbearable. It also caused the fingers of my right hand to go numb from time to time. I looked at that as a problem that could potentially hurt me down the road, seeing as I was right handed.

Perjah and her daughter Brittany moved into the mini-mansion along with me, and I was glad they had because I had grown familiar with them being around me, especially, Perjah. Apart of me was somewhat dependent on her presence. Seeing her kept me calm and motivated mw to get better so I could place us within a better position to succeed.

It had been four days since I'd left the hospital. I had just finished an intense exerting workout when Perjah came into the basement with a plate if fried chicken, white rice, pinto beans, and a sweet slice of Jiffy Mix cornbread. She had a glass of grape soda pop and a smile on her face. "I waited for as long as I could before I came down to bring you this food. I know you working all hard and stuff but I was missing you like crazy. Here." She handed me the plate and kissed my lips, sucking all over them.

Perjah was 5'5" tall and caramel skinned with light freckles on her face that made her look so damn sexy to me. She had brown eyes, dimples, and weighed about 125 pounds. She was slightly bow-legged and had the body of a goddess. I cared about her a lot. My feelings for her had developed faster than I'd planned.

I finished kissing her lips and looked down at the food with a smile on my face. "Baby, thank you for slaving over that stove, but, damn, it ain't nothing but carbs and saturated fats on this plate. What you trying to do; get me chunky or something?"

She shook her head. "I just wanna make sure that you're eating. It looks like you've already lost too much weight. I can't allow that. I'm cool with you getting all ripped and stuff, but when I first saw you, you were real muscular. I thought you were one of the sexiest men I'd ever seen in my entire life. With your light brown eyes and golden skin complexion. Umph! I'm trying to get you back to that weight."

I can't lie and say I didn't feel somewhat offended. I felt like she was trying to say that I wasn't as attractive as I had been to her in the past. That made me feel some type of way. "Oh, so you saying I ain't doing it for you no more?"

She took the plate out of my hand and stepped into my face again. She took my hands and placed them on her big booty. "Nah, I ain't saying that. You should already know how I feel about you. Who was standing at your side when you opened your eyes for the first time in that hospital room?" She licked my lips.

I slid my hands under her short nightgown and rubbed all over her hot skin. I slid my hand between her thigh gap, and the sides of my fingers grazed against her sex lips, slightly opening them. I took the middle finger and slid it into her hot hole, stroking it in and out.

"Umm, you think you strong enough to work on me real quick?" She sucked on my neck and humped backward into my finger. Cocked her legs open and moaned into my mouth.

"You was there, baby, and hell yeah I'm strong enough to hit this pussy. All you gotta do is find out." I snaked two fingers into her gap, running them in and out of her.

She pushed me back into the wall and dropped down to her knees. She pulled my piece out of my boxers and stroked it in her little hand. "I been missing you so much, baby. I swear I have." She ran her tongue across her thick, juicy lips before sucking my head into her mouth. At the same time, she pulled the skin all the way back on my stack and sucked on my penis head as if it was a chicken bone. She looked into my eyes and swallowed me whole, gagging just a little bit.

I grabbed a hand full of her wavy hair and guided her up and down my pole. My eyes rolled into the back of my head. I stood on my tippy toes, pumping in and out of her hot mouth. It felt like a closed, sweltering fist. "Damn, Perjah. Damn, ma, welcome home to me."

She sucked me with blazing speed, pumping my piece as she did her thing. She'd stop, lick all over the head, then suck me back into her mouth, groaning all over my tool. It was feeling so good that I didn't know how long I could last. There was nothing like watching a dime piece give you head, in my opinion. She was so bad that looking in her face had the cum bubbling up inside of me. I was on the verge of splashing. My dick started to jump all crazy like.

Perjah stood up and pulled her night gown above her waist. She ran her fingers through her shaved cat and opened the lips. She slipped a finger deep into herself, pulled it out and sucked it into her mouth. "Umm, ain't you trying to taste me too?" She placed her pedicured feet up on my weight bench.

I kneeled in front of her and bit into her thick thigh. I squeezed it in my hand. It was chunky and hot. She was so thick that it sent shivers through me. I wanted her so bad, but first I just had to taste her essence. We'd only gotten together one time previous to this one, and I remembered how sweet she'd tasted on my tongue. I stuck my face in her gap and sucked her sex lips into my mouth, slurping her juices while I held that big booty in my hands.

"Uhh! Yes. Yes. Tristian!" She humped into my face, bumping her clit against my nose. It left a streak of juices. She smelled so good to me. Her scent was intoxicating.

I held her lips apart and slid my tongue as deep into her as I could. It forced its way into her box, darting in and out of her, before I added two fingers. "Cum for me, Perjah. Cum all on my tongue. I need to taste you." I encouraged her.

She grabbed the back of my head and forced me deeper into her gap. She popped her back and tilted her face toward the ceiling. "Tristian. Oooh, Tristian. It's so good. It's so good. Uhh, baby."

I got to making all kinds of loud, nasty noises as I ate that thang. My fingers shot in and out of her at full speed. Her juices dripped off of my wrist and slid down my forearm. I nipped at her clit, before sucking it like a berry.

She screamed and bucked against me. "I'm cumming, baby. Ooh-wee, I'm cumming. Uhh-yes!" She stuffed my face between her thighs and started to shake so hard that she buckled against me.

I continued to eat her with her juices running down my neck. She stood up and I bent her over the weight bench. Opened her ass cheeks, and stuck my tongue into her crinkle, worming it around inside of her. I had to appreciate that big booty. A woman as thick as her deserved A-1 attention. I licked all over each cheek and sucked on the meat of them.

She arched her back and looked over her shoulder at me biting on her bottom lip. "Uh, what are you doing to me, Tristian? What are you doing, baby?"

I sucked up and down her thick thighs and was back to eating her kitty from the back, holding her pussy lips wide open so I could attack that clitoris. Her cat was a lil' darker than her actual complexion, and it was sexy to me. A clear gelatinous string of juice dripped out of it and ran down her thigh.

I smacked that big ass and stood up behind her, rubbing all over that round blessing. There were a few stretch marks that decorated its surface. What she may have considered her imperfections were actually traces of perfection to me. I dropped my boxers and trailed my piece up and down her slit, wetting my helmet in the process. Her hot essence oozed on to the top of it and seemed to beg me to enter her. "Do you want me, baby?"

She moaned and ran her tongue all over her lips. "Yes. I need you, Tristian. Give me some of that pipe. Now!" She shouted and spread her pretty feet further apart.

I smacked her ass and watched her cheeks jiggle along with her thighs. I slid two fingers into her box from the back and worked them in and out of her. I liked to watch her lips open and close around them. I was obsessed with the sight, scent, and taste of pussy. Hers was so fat that it looked like a mini booty. While my fingers ran in and out of her I slid my tongue back into her asshole.

"Oh my God, baby. Oh my God. You doing too much. You doing way too much." She moaned, reaching under her belly and tweaking her clitoris.

I watched her pinch it and pull on it as if it were a long nipple. Her scent rose out of her hole and wafted right up my nose. It smelled like strawberry and pussy in the air.

"Give me some, now, Tristian. Put it in me. Hurry up, baby, before Brittany wake up."

I stood back up and slowly slid into her hot box from the back. I was so hard that veins were all over my pipe. It looked as if it were on steroids. As the first few inches passed through her lips, my entire body began to tingle. "Shit."

Perjah tossed her head back and moaned. "Yes, baby. Now hit that cat. Hit this pussy hard, Tristian. I've missed you so much." She slammed back into me, forcing my entire pipe to travel deep into her.

I grabbed a hold of her hips and used them for grip. With ten long and hard strokes I was in rhythm. I was sliding in and out of her at full speed while I groaned and whimpered just a lil' bit because that pussy was good. Perjah was blessed.

It was like the good lord above took his time while crafting her hot pocket. It fit me so perfectly. It was tight, but not so tight that it was uncomfortable for me. It was just right, and I was stroking that cat like a champ. It sounded like somebody was in the room clapping their hands every time our skins slammed into one another's.

"Uh, uh, yes, yes, yes. Tristian. You. Got me, baby. Uh, yes, you got me locked down. You got me locked down, Daddy!" Her arm straps had fallen off of her shoulders. Because of this, her B cup breasts had worked themselves out into the open. Both nipples were erect and juicy. Her titties bounced on her small frame as I rocked her from behind like a gangsta on business.

I grabbed a handful of her hair again, leaned over her back and sucked her tongue into my mouth while we sexed like jack rabbits.

"I'm about to cum, Daddy. I'm about to cum again. So hard. So hard. Uh-yes!" She slammed back into me ten hard times and squealed.

I sped up the pace as I felt my nut building deep within me. I stroked and stroked, plunging deeper and deeper watching my dick go in and out of her pussy. I watched her ass cheeks shaking and it became too much. I smacked that fat booty, rubbed all over it and came deep within her channel. Squirt after squirt until I fell against her, sucking on the back of her neck.

* * *

After we showered, I carried her upstairs to the master bedroom where I laid her on the bed, before I crawled on to it myself. I took the remote, and turned on a piece by Neyo called "A Good Man." After all that sexing, I was feeling like I needed to connect with her on an emotional level. I needed to know where her head was because the next stages of my life were about to become extremely dangerous. I needed to know if she was going to ride beside me while I reigned as king, or if she was going to take the high road. I would respect whatever decision she chose.

I started by pulling her on top of me naked. She straddled my body and laid her head on my chest while I rubbed all over her booty. "Baby, I got some questions for you and I need for you to answer them from your heart, okay?"

She yawned and kissed my nipple, running her hand along my left shoulder. She adjusted and laid her head on my collarbone until I moved her off of it when a severe pain shot up and down it. "What do you want to know, baby?"

"Well, it's in my DNA to be king of my family. Before my father fell into the state that he is in now, he handed over the reigns of the family to me. I have to step into his shoes and elevate the Vegas, against all odds. That means that I might have to do a lot of killing, and cut throat type shit in order to stay on top. I need to know if you gon' roll with me. If you do, I swear I'll be one hunnit to you. I'll hold you down like no other and make sure that you and Brittany never want or need for anything as long as I'm alive. But if you think that you can't be that woman that stays by my side, then I'll still do what I can for you from a distance."

Perjah sat all the way up and placed her small hands on my chest. Her thick thighs were on each side of me. They were so distracting. She brushed her long hair out of her face and flipped it behind her. "Baby, even if I wanted to ride beside you and hold you down the way that I am supposed to, how could I? I have to take care of Brittany. What about her?"

I sat up with my back against the headboard. "Brittany will have the best care that money can provide. I'll still do my part to make sure that she has me. I love her, and I just want to insure that she's never placed in harm's way, or needs for anything in life. I'll have armed guards around the both of you from here on out. I guess what I'm trying to say is that I want to be with you. I've been crazy about you ever since the first time I saw you in that waiting room. I knew that one day you'd be my diamond. I need for you to give me the chance to shine you, and keep you polished, tucked safe and sound in a palace of your choosing. I wanna take you on foreign trips and upgrade your lifestyle just a little bit. Maybe we can put a few businesses behind you so you can produce your own wealth. What ever your dreams are, allow me to help you to bring them into fruition."

"Tristian, all of that sounds so good, but won't it be dangerous? Who's to say that something bad won't happen to you and then where would that leave me and her?" She rubbed my chest.

I continued to cuff that ass. I pulled her closer to me. Her bald kitty singed my stomach muscles. I had visions of licking up and down it again. I took a deep breath and exhaled slowly. "Yeah, it's going to be dangerous, but I need for you to trust me. I won't let anything happen to you or Brittany. I just want to give you guys the best life that I possibly can. I need to. I yearn to, baby. Please." I pulled her to me and kissed her lips.

She closed her eyes and kissed me back. She slid her tongue into my mouth. I sucked on it and swallowed her spit. I felt it slide down my throat and into my belly.

"How do you know we'll be safe, baby? How do you know that Showbiz or your other brother won't try and bring harm against us? Your mother says that they're dirty and rotten to their very core."

I held her face in my hands. "What you have to understand is that me and them have the same DNA. There is nothing inside of them that's not inside of me. I have only chosen to let that rotten part of me remain dormant. But not anymore. In order to survive in this game I gotta get grimy, ma, but that ain't got nothin' to do with you or Brittany. I'll put y'all up in our own home down in Miami. Keep it guarded by some of the deadliest men that are loyal to me and only me. I'll take care of you, Perjah. You and Birittany. And put you in a position so that you will be able to do for yourself. That's my word and promise to you and her."

Perjah climbed off of my lap and got out of the bed. Her chunky ass cheeks jiggled as she paced on thick thighs. Her naked breasts bounced. She looked like a naked goddess placed in the garden of Eden strictly for me. I had to keep her close. I was infatuated with this beauty.

"Tristian, you are making things so hard for me. Every fiber of my being is telling me to stand by your side and enter this war with you as your queen. But then there is the mother and more responsible side of myself that is screaming for me to put my daughter first. To take her out of harm's way. The night that you were hit up for the second time, your brothers could have very well chosen to come after me and my daughter. Had they done so they could have very well killed us and thought nothing of it. From what I hear, Showbiz is lethal. He won't hesitate to kill a female just as quick as he would a dude. Flex's birthday party proved that to us, am I right?"

I nodded. She had a point, and I didn't see no use in trying to persuade her otherwise. "My brother is a beast. But so am I. I'd rather die than to allow anything to happen to you or Brittany. I need you to trust me. Give me the chance. Let me show you that I have things under control. I want you in my life, Perjah. I gotta have you by my side."

She looked up into my eyes and bit into her bottom lip. She shook her head and smiled. "I don't know what I'm gon' do about you. I can tell you're going to wind up being my downfall one of these days. I'm so freaking attracted to you already." She sighed out loud, wrapped her arms around my lower back, then laid her head on my chest. "Give me some time to think about it, Tristian. Let me mull some things over. I know without a shadow of a doubt that I want to be with you. I can tell that you're a good man and you care about me and my daughter. That's says a lot about your overall character."

I knew that my life was about to take off in so many directions that I was going to need a consistent person in my circle that really cared about me beyond the lifestyle. I was sure that Perjah was going to be that one. Even though she'd not given me a direct answer, I was banking on her being by my side.

Chapter 3

It was three days later and I'd been summoned to one of my father's mansions out on Staten Island. It was a white bricked, three story mansion with a driveway about a hundred feet long. The driveway led into a six-car garage. My Pops had it packed with two Rolls Royce, a Ferrari, a Hummer, one all black Rafi, and another that was red. He ordered for one of his cars to pick up. When I got there, I noted that Showbiz's Benz truck was parked in the driveway. I felt myself getting heated right away. I situated the vest on my chest and made sure that the .40 Glock in the small of my back was safely tucked. I was silently praying to God and asking him to give me the strength to refrain from knocking my brother's head off at my pops' pad.

I saw visions of the police lining his body with chalk after I'd dumped a whole clip in his face, only to have reloaded and do the same thing to Miguel. In my mind they were both my enemies until I got to the bottom of finding out which one of the chumps had shot me up.

When I made it inside of my father's house, one of his bodyguards led me into the den where I found Showbiz, Miguel, Shapiro, and my father's brother, Javier, sitting.

When Showbiz saw me he stood up with a smile on his face. "Oh shit, I see you put a whole new meaning to the phrase walking dead, Tristian." He laughed then curled his lip. He was dressed in a black and red Burberry suit. His wavy hair was pulled back into a ponytail. He wore Ray Bans glasses on his face.

Miguel looked up to him and laughed. "That fool won't be breathin' for long. Shit, even Steph Curry miss a shot every now and then. Nah'mean?" He pulled his nose and sniffed loudly.

I grunted and nodded. "Showbiz, sit yo' punk ass down. I'll deal with you later. I got somethin' for yo ass too, Miguel. I'm tired of whooping yo' ass. You just don't get it, do you?"

Showbiz scrunched his face and made his way in my direction as if he was going to do something. "You know what? If I gotta take yo' head off right here before Pops come down then so be it. The lines are drawn in the sand anyway. What's good?"

I'd had it up to here with him. I took the Glock out of the small of my back and got ready to cock and buss his bitch ass when my father entered into the room in a wheelchair. The sight of him in such a hobbled state was enough to soften me. He was also hooked up to an oxygen machine. My mind was completely blown. I was wondering how he'd fallen so low in just the amount of time that I'd been in the hospital.

"Mijo, put that gun back in your waist. And you, Jaunito, have a fucking seat. Have some respect for my home, or do you think I am dead already?" He said all of these things to us in Spanish.

My brother's real name was Jaunito. He was named after my father's mother, Jaunita.

I slid the gun back into the small of my back and pulled my polo over it. "That's my apologies, Pop. Sometimes I let my anger get the better of me."

Showbiz sucked his teeth. "You ain't on shit, Tristian. One of these days I'ma make you use that muhfucka." He pulled out his chair and plopped down into it, never taking his eyes off of me.

The bodyguard wheeled my father to the head of the table and stood behind him. My father closed his eyes for a second and then opened them. They were blood shot and watery. He swallowed and ran his fingers through his graying hair. "I have three sons that are to carry on the name of the Vegas. Seeds of my loins. Yet when I look across this table at the three of you all I see are enemies. All of you are so in a rush to be seated upon this throne, but I seriously doubt if any of you know what you're in for." He took the oxygen machine and adjusted the nozzle, placing the mask on his face for thirty second, inhaling deeply with his eyes closed, then he sat it back on his lap.

I could hear him wheezing and gasping for air. It scared me. I didn't like seeing my old man in that state. Because he was my father I started to wonder if one day I'd be in the same physically ailing predicament he was in. I had always been one to be very particular about my health. My father had strong genes. I was worried about what all he'd passed down to me.

He cleared his throat. "I called you all here today with the intentions of finally crowning, Tristian, as head of the Vega family, but then when I walk into the room, I see that you are about to pull a gun out on your brother. To do what with, I have no idea. But I can only imagine. That behavior is not the type of behavior that I want running this family. However, it's been brought to my attention, Juanito, that you may have been responsible for the try on your brother's life." He started to cough before placing the mask back over his face and inhaling.

Showbiz stood up. "Say, Pops, muhfuckas lying to you. If I was the one pulling the trigger on that nigga I'd a killed him. You already know what the streets of New York say about me. I'm a certified killer." He mugged me and smiled. "Whoever hit Tristian up ain't know what they were doing. I'm the one that gave him the vest. I would have aimed straight for his fucking head; word is bond." He sat back in his seat.

I nodded and mugged at first him, and then Miguel. My little brother Miguel's face had turned a beet red. He refused to make eye contact with Showbiz. That told me that he was the man behind the trigger. At least that's how I was thinking at that time.

"Witnesses say the truck that pulled up on me was a Benz truck. Not just any Benz truck either. Your Benz truck, Showbiz. So, it was either you, or that pussy sitting right there next to you!" I hollered, slamming my hand on the table.

"Nigga, don't throw me in the mix. Whatever y'all got going on is between y'all. I ain't got nothing to do with it." Miguel said, refusing to look over at me. He looked as guilty as a cat caught with a canary in its mouth.

I made up my mind right then that I was gon' have to knock his head off. You see, Miguel was my father's youngest son. He was also full-blooded Cuban like Showbiz. Even though he and I were paternal brothers, we'd never gotten along because he was a racist. Every time he got into it with a Black person, he'd wind up calling them a nigger, or something worst. I ain't like that shit, so every time I got the chance to whoop his ass I did exactly that. The last time I'd knocked him out in front of his pregnant girlfriend and he'd vowed revenge. I never took him seriously, but I saw then that I had to.

"Yo, I'm telling you now, Pop, I ain't accepting no more slugs from nobody. I don't care if they're blood or not. Word is bond, somebody gon' pay for those sins." I stood up and turned toward Miguel and Showbiz. "You niggas was man enough to pull them triggers but you ain't man enough to tell me which one of you did it? What's good?"

Showbiz laughed and kicked his feet up on the table. "Pop, tell this soft ass nigga to sit down and shut up. We got business to handle today. Life is too short. You know that more than anybody."

I felt like he'd taken a dig at my old man on the sly. I got ready to rush his bitch ass when Shapiro grabbed my arm. "Tristian, it's not worth it. Have a seat. Today is your day."

I continued to mug Showbiz and nodded. "Yeah, you're right." I sat down and interlocked my fingers.

My father took the oxygen mask off of his face and sat it back into his lap. "I built this family from the ground up. It was my hard work, blood, sweat and tears that has gotten us to this point. I started back in Havana working the sugar cane fields alongside my father. I worked twelve hours a day in the hot sun, and then another eight in the factory where the sugar was granulated. Back then the Vegas were so poor that we were barely able to afford a one room hut that fourteen of my siblings were forced to live in. There was only one room and no indoor plumbing. We'd dig a hole in the back of the house and that's where we did our business. We made the best of it and we were supposed to be thankful for it. But you know what? I never was." He put the oxygen mask back over his face, inhaling deeply before placing it back on to his lap. "Ever since I was old enough to understand the struggles of the Vegas, I've yearned to take our family to the next level. I always felt that the Vegas are supposed to be rich, mighty, and powerful. The Vegas are supposed to be the family that rules the world. We are better than the Kennedys. Greater than the Bushs. For our bloodline the sky is the limit." He coughed into his fist and beat on his chest.

I adjusted myself in my chair. I was trying to see where my father was going with everything. When it came to his speeches it was imperative that I understood the meaning behind them because there was always a message. I looked over at Showbiz and saw that he had his phone lowered below the table, texting away with his thumbs. Miguel looked as if he were paying attention but with him I could never say for sure.

"Pop, you saying all this to say what?" Showbiz asked, looking up from his phone.

My father frowned and shook his head. "I'm saying this to say that nothing is given in this family. You have to earn everything that you have. I have made it too easy on you boys. I've allowed for you to live in the lap of luxury and you have given up nothing for the cause. You have top of the line cars and well-built homes. I placed five hundred thousand dollars into your bank accounts before you were old enough to walk, and what have you given back to me? Not a damn thing." He snapped and broke into a fit of coughs once again.

I sat upright. I was starting to dread where my father was about to take things. "Pop, you said the deal was that the first son that brought you fifteen million dollars that would be contributed to Senator Grant's campaign, you'd place him on your throne and surrender the family over to that son. Now it's starting to sound like you're about to switch that up. That ain't fair." I said.

He shook his head. "Cool your jets, Mijo, I never said that I was going back on my word. I was simply speaking from my heart. Had your brother allowed for me to finish I would have been able to get there. But I will now. Sons, I've called you here to keep my word. I want to say that after I take my last breath, Tristian, you will officially become the head of the Vega family, both here and back on our native island of Cuba. Shapiro, it is your job to train him the right way and bring him up to be the business man that you've witnessed me being. Javier, you will take Tristian back home and introduce him to the family on the island. Show him the business and how the operation works. Maybe if he's able to understand where we come from, he'll wheel more of a connection and it will inspire him to take our family to the next level."

Javier nodded. "Right away, Boss."

"Tristian, for as long as I am alive I will be your mentor. I will give you my wisdom. It is my hope that you will soak it up and never take it for granted. The fate of the Vegas are on your shoulders now." He wiggled out of the wheelchair and limped over to me. Took a safety pin out of his inside pocket and poked his finger. "Turn around, Mijo, and face me."

I did as I was told.

My father pricked his finger, grabbed my head and kissed me on the forehead before placing his blood on it, crossing it with the sign of the crucifix. "May God be with you on all of your endeavors and may He help you to elevate our bloodline."

Showbiz jumped up and slammed his hand on the table. "This some bullshit. You've always favored that fuck nigga because of his Black ass mama. You think I didn't know that?" He spat.

My father kissed me on both of cheeks and ignored him. "I love you, son. I trust you, son. Go in the ways of me, your father." He continued.

"You think I need this shit. You think I need yo' fucking throne. I am New York. I got twenty million dollars at my disposal. This nigga will never rule me. I'd rather die first."

I mugged this disrespectful ass nigga and wanted to get up and buck his ass a couple times. I was tired of him coming at my pops like he wasn't our king. My old man was already battling some serious health issues and Showbiz acted like he didn't give a flying fuck. I had to handle his ass in a raw fashion. Blood brother aside, I was feeling like fuck this nigga.

My father ended by kissing my forehead. He coughed into his fist again and stumbled back into his wheelchair. The bodyguard came behind him and pushed him back to the head of the table. "Juanito, if you were not my first-born son I'd have your balls cut off and fed to you. You're not equipped to be king of this family. You're a hot head, self-centered, egotistical prick. You're tough, but you're weak. No peasant will sit upon my throne, DNA or not. You disgust me, and I have a mind to get out of this chair, and—" He grabbed his chest and tensed up before falling out of it and shaking like crazy.

I rushed out of my chair was to his side, even before the bodyguard that was standing behind him could catch him. I tapped the side of his face. "Pop? Pop? What's the matter, man?"

He shook as if he were having a seizure. His eyes rolled into the back of his head. He opened his mouth but only gagging noises escaped from it.

Shapiro pulled be back and kneeled to give him CPR. "Tristian, go and call his personal nurse. She's upstairs in her room. Hurry, kid." He ordered me as he began the chest compressions.

I rushed out of the room with tears in my eyes. I took the steps two at a time until I was standing in front of the nurse's door, beating on it like crazy. "Pilar! Pilar, come quick! My father is having a heart attack of some sort!" I hollered to her in Spanish.

She rushed out of the room with no shirt. I could tell that she was changing clothes because she was in just her bra and a slip.

When we got back into the den my father was laid on his back. His face was the color of blue. His eyes were closed and he was unmoving.

Pilar dropped beside him and placed her ear on his chest, then raised her head and shook it. "He's gone. Senor Vega is gone."

I broke into a fit of tears with my chest heaving. I felt sick to my stomach. I was dizzy and my vision was a little hazy. I leaned down and kissed my old man on both of his cheeks. "I love you, Pop. I love you with all of my heart."

Miguel kneeled across from me with tears running down his cheeks. "Ay, Papa. Why did you have to go already, Papa?" He questioned, laying his head on his chest.

Showbiz came and stood over him with his lip curled. "Tsk! Even the Lord above know he made a stupid ass decision. That's why he took his life, ASAP." He sucked his teeth loudly and shook his head. "I don't give a fuck what yo' dead ass say, old man. It's only one king of the Vegas, and that's me. Rest in hell, Pops. This bitch nigga that you chose will be there real soon." He said this looking down at me.

I bounced up and picked his ass up in the air and slammed him on the long oak wood table so hard that the leg popped from under it and crashed into the walls on each side. I straddled his body and rained one punch down on his ass after the other, Hitting him as hard as I could in his mouth and jaw. "You. Bitch. Ass. Nigga. How. Dare. You. Disrespect. My—"

Miguel picked up a lamp and crashed it on the back of my head, knocking me off of Showbiz. It hurt so bad that for a few seconds I was unable to move my limbs.

Showbiz jumped on top of me and punched me so many times that he knocked me clear out. When I woke up, I saw two of my father's bodyguards pulling him off of me. They also had Miguel in a full Nelson whilst he kicked his legs like crazy.

I staggered to my feet with blood dripping off of my chin. My jaw felt like it was broken and so did my nose. I made a move to rush Showbiz's ass and was snatched up by my buff ass uncle, Javier. "Calm down, Mijo. We have to make some sense of all of this. You have to keep your head. Now is not the time for disfunction." He said this in Spanish.

Showbiz broke away from the guards and spat at their feet. "I'm the muthafucking king now. It's my birthright. That doped up old man ain't know what the fuck he was talking about." He wiped blood from his mouth with the back of his hand and looked at it, then laughed. He mugged me and nodded. "The throne is mine, fuck nigga. Anybody that follows you is an enemy to me and my empire. That goes for you too, Shapiro. I'm giving you and Javier until the funeral to decide which son you're going to honor as king. Decide wisely. The consequences are certain to be dire. Let's go, Miguel!"

They both mugged me as they left the room. With each step that they took my heart felt like it was getting colder and colder. This was the day that I honestly felt I became a lunatic. This was the day that my heart turned as cold as ice. I knew that in order to survive as head of the Vegas I was going to have to step that killer part of me all the way up, and in honor of my father. I aint have no problem doing it.

Chapter 4

My Pops was buried a week later. Our family held a very private funeral for him. The only people that were invited per his request were his sons and my sisters, Brooklyn and Alissa. The ceremony was held in the back of his Mansion in Bayside, and out of the three sons that were invited I was the only one that showed up. I saw that as the ultimate disrespect. After everything that my father had done for us, my brothers couldn't even respect him enough to say their good byes. That pissed me off.

After he was buried I kneeled beside his grave and said a small prayer. I prayed for God to accept him into heaven. I prayed for forgiveness on his behalf. I also prayed that all of his strength would be passed on to me. That I would make a great king and be able to honor the Vega name that he'd passed down to me.

While I was on one knee, Shapiro waited until I crossed my body with the crucifix before he came over and placed his hand on my shoulder. "Come on, kid. Unfortunately we don't have any more time to waste. The Gómezes have officially brought about their first act of war. While you were here, they put more than a thousand bullet holes in your brownstone before sending a cocktail bomb through the window. At this time your house is completely engulfed in flames."

I stood up. "But I don't stay there anymore. All that's left are my clothes and some electronic items.

They must've gotten the wrong intel." I dusted off my pants.

Shapiro shook his head. "You've got a lot to learn, kid. Bruno is a very wise guy. He has a lot of money and I'm sure that he knows that it's not your primary residence any longer, but it was just his way of sending a message to the family. I believe he knows that you've been crowned king. This is his way of saying your reign will be short lived. We have to respond right away. It'll set the tone. These small attacks have a way of revealing the character of the man that you're opposing. I say we hit him hard, and fast. But of course, the ultimate decision will be up to you."

I nodded. "Let's do this shit. If Bruno wanna kick it off with me right away, I ain't got no problem getting my hands dirty."

"That's what I like to hear, Boss. It is always good to out-think your enemy, but when things like this happen so prematurely you have to set brains aside and come with fire power."

* * *

I stepped into the basement of my father's mansion and was shocked at what I saw. It was an hour after the burial, and Javier had called my phone and asked me to meet him at my father's mansion, along with Shapiro. When I walked in the basement I saw that there were about fifteen men surrounding the oak wood table. They looked to be both Cuban and Black. They were dressed in army fatigue pants and black leather boots that laced up nearly to their knees. They wore black wife beaters and stood at attention when I stepped into the room. The long oak wood table was covered with all kinds of fully automatic weapons. There was also a crate of grenades. My eyes were bugged out of my head, but I had to play it cool.

Javier greeted me with an outstretched hand. He spoke all of his words in Spanish. "Nephew, once again I am sorry for your loss. I know that your father is looking down on you in this moment. With that being said, we have to attack the Gómezes right away to set the precedent. I say we hit their restaurant on Dwight and Verona Street over in Brooklyn. What do you think?" He asked me and waved his hand over the table full of weapons as if asking me to pick one.

Shapiro stepped forward. "It's a smaller more intimate setting. I think it'll get attention, but if we really want to make a splash, we target one of his children's homes just as he's targeted yours, Tristian. It almost has to be an eye for an eye. It's the only thing that crazed bosses like him understand. He's drunk with power and dead set on enacting his revenge for the deaths of his two sons. Although their deaths have never been confirmed, have they?" He looked over to, Javier.

"The word back on the island is that the sons of Chico Vega are responsible for their deaths."

"Let me ask you both a question. If I give the order for their restaurant to be shot up, what kind of backlash are we looking at here?"

Javier shrugged again. "Well, kid, war is war. They shoot at us, we have to return fire or we're viewed as pushovers. Our family will not be able to survive in a climate where we are viewed as soft. The

Vegas are known for going at their enemies hard. Chico died with a body count in the thousands. You will as well, Tristian. It's the only way."

"Yeah, let me worry about the backlash, kid. For now, you need to introduce yourself to the troops, then get out there and show them that you are just as much of an animal as they are." He pat me on the back and kind of pushed me toward the table.

Javier spoke up. Once again, every word that came out of his mouth was in Spanish. "Okay, listen up. This is Senor Vega. He is now the king of the Vegas. You will honor him as such. I expect you to give him your loyalties just as you did his father. He is going to introduce himself, and let you know how things are going to go from here on out. You will remain at attention during the process. If you understand me, you will clap your boots together."

They all clapped their boots together and stomped their feet. It appeared that they were looking off in the distance, but I'd heard that those in the military while being spoken too by their superior were supposed to find a place on the wall and drill a hole through it with their eyes. I didn't know what the purpose of that was, but this is what these men were doing.

I decided to channel my father's spirit. I spoke to them in a broken Spanish dialect. "Gentlemen, let me say that it will be a pleasure working alongside you. You will always get my upmost respect at all times. All I ask is for your loyalty. In exchange I will make sure that you and your families are well taken care of, both here and back home in Cuba. There is nothing that you can't come to me about. And because of your fight for me and my bloodline, there is nothing that I would not do for you, on your behalf. I am a man of devotion. If you are devoted to me, I will be the same to you. With that being said, I expect you to be killers. Cold-hearted savages that murder for the blood of the Vegas. I will not take kindly to cowards, or betrayal in this outfit. You will be murdered with no remorse. Do I may myself clear?"

They were silent until my uncle stood beside me. "Does he make himself clear?" he hollered.

"Sir, yes, sir!" They responded in unison.

I slammed my hand on the table and a Mach .90 fell off of it and onto the floor. "I am in charge here. You respond to me louder than you do anyone else. Now, do I make myself clear!" I hollered picking up an AK47 and slamming a clip into it.

"Sir, yes, sir!" They returned and stomped their right foot on the ground.

* * *

Thirty minutes later, Javier loaded up five of the men into a black Ford Ecoline while him and myself, along with two armed guards jumped in a black Hummer with me in the passenger's seat. I had a hundred round clip sticking out of my AK47. In New York we called it a Bin Laden because he had been notorious for being filmed with them jokers. I was dressed in all black, with a black ski mask in my lap, ready to be pulled over my head when the time was right. We'd decided to hit up Gómezes that were out in Brooklyn. It was conveniently located a few blocks away from the Red Hook Houses that the Gómezes at one point had taken over. That was before Showbiz imposed his will on the drug infested housing projects.

I wanted to make a statement to Bruno Gomez right away that I wasn't going to be the one he could fuck with. I understood that in order for me to be respected as a prominent drug lord that I'd also had to be a killer. I couldn't be afraid to get my hands dirty. Most families survived by preying on the weak. I could never allow for the Vegas to be looked upon as weak. I was the king. The world would soon feel my wrath. I was certain of that.

We pulled a block away from the Gómezes, at about nine o'clock the same night of my Pop's funeral. I slid the mask over my face and directed Javier to pull about a hundred yards away from the back of the parking lot. He did just that, and I jumped out of the Hummer with my Bin Laden in my hands. The five soldiers hopped out of the black Ecoline and fell in tow behind me. We jogged through the night and into the parking lot. I'd already given the order that the plan was to tear the establishment to shreds. They were to avoid hitting any innocent patrons. But were expected to annihilate any threats on sight.

The moon was full in the sky. It was a hot night, but not really that humid. The mask was sticky on my face, full of sweat. I wiped a bit of it from my eyes before throwing open the door and walking inside with my fully automatic pointed ahead of me. There was an older Cuban man waiting just a few feet from the door with a white towel draped over his right arm. His eyes got as big as paper plates when he saw us file inside. He pushed a female waitress in our direction and took off running.

I caught her and slung her to the floor. "Stay down!" I ordered, aimed at the fleeing man and pulled the trigger. *Boom. Boom. Boom. Boom. Boom.* My bullets tore into the wall in front of him.

He fell to the floor, reached in his waistband and aimed a gun, but it was too late. Now I was looking through my scope and chopping his ass down. *Boom. Boom. Boom. Boom.* The bullets punched massive holes into his chest and left his insides hanging out of him.

My troops took off in every direction, bussing their assault rifles. The patrons in the restaurant began to scream and holler as they dropped to the floor and hid under their tables.

Boom. Boom. Boom. Boom. I let more bullets loose. "Hey, Bruno! Where the fuck are you, pussy! You're looking for me?" I shouted making my way through the establishment.

I could hear my troops' guns barking. Shells tinkled on the floor. Plaster flew from the walls and left big white clouds of smoke. The scent of gunpowder was heavy in the air.

Two men in white aprons came from the back of the kitchen with shotguns in their hands. They kneeled and pulled their triggers. One of them shot one of my heavy-set hittas. He flew backward and over a table after hollering at the top of his lungs.

I ducked behind the pew where the hostess had been standing, kneeled, and zoomed in to the two shooters with the use of my scope. I lined one of them up and pulled the trigger.*Boom. Boom. Boom.* The bullets attacked his neck. He threw his shotgun into the air and flew backward. His partner stood up and bussed two times in my direction before my troops filled him with so many holes that he slid down the wall looking like a dead ass version of human Swiss cheese.

I smiled and nodded. "Hey, Bruno! You wanna fuck with me! You want some of the king, muthafucka!" I hollered, kicking in the door to the kitchen, finding all of the workers laying on their stomachs with their hands over their heads. "Where the fuck is Bruno?" I hollered.

A Spanish woman about the age of forty scooted backward on her ass. She shook her head. "Bruno isn't here. I swear!" She screamed in Spanish.

My troops filed into the kitchen on high alert. I grabbed a handful of the woman's hair and pulled her to her feet. She struggled against me. "Bitch, listen to me. You tell Bruno that if he wants a war, a war is what he'll get, but I am ten times worse than my father. You get that!"

She nodded. "Okay. Yes, please, don't kill me." She started to shake so bad that I feared her having a heart attack.

I pushed her back to the floor and looked around the dirty kitchen. "Tear this bitch up, and let's be out!" I ordered.

I stood by and watched my troops shoot the kitchen into shreds. Their bullets slammed into the big pots and pans, knocking them from the hanging racks they were on. Dishes were shattered. The walls received big holes in them. Bullet holes filled the refrigerator door and all of the dry goods. By the time we left Gomez's we'd left more than a thousand rounds of ammunition in the place. I was sure that word would get back to Bruno Gomez. I needed it to. If it was a war that he wanted with the Vega family, then I would give him exactly that and so much more.

Chapter 5

A month later, Senator Grant took office. My mother woke me up bright and early this day, beating on the door to my master bedroom. I was laid on my back with Perjah halfway on top of me. Her thick thigh was around my waist. I could feel the heat from her box breathing on me.

"I think you should answer it." She yawned into her hand.

I placed my hands on her round ass and slid her from the top of me. "Ma, what's good? I'm still sleep. It's only five in the morning." I was super irritated and wondering how she'd managed to get into my crib when I had four bodyguards that were supposed to be on point at all times.

"Tristian, you get yo' ass out of that bed and get down these stairs. I need to talk to you. Hurry up, you got ten minutes!" I could hear her feet stomping down the hall.

"Damn, baby, your mother is something else. The sun ain't came up yet and she already on yo' ass. It sucks to be you." She smiled and rolled onto her side.

I flipped her on her back and straddled her, kissing her juicy lips. "Baby, I wanna do something special for you today. Anything you want, or anything you wanna do we can do it. I know you been cooped up in this mansion for a few weeks. That gotta get boring." I kissed her again.

She moaned. "Yeah, it do, but I been handling my business on line, trying to snatch up one of these degrees. I guess I do feel like getting my fingers and toes done. I'm pretty sure Brittany would like that as well. We can probably get a full body massage for the both of us too. As far as everything else go, we'll play that by ear. Is that cool?"

I opened her thighs all the way and had a mouth full of her pussy. My tongue slid up and down her slit hungrily. Her juices dripped into my mouth. I slurped and kissed her clit. "Hell, yeah, Boo, that sound good to me. It's whatever you like. Maybe after you splurge a lil' bit you'll be able to tell me if you've made up our mind about holding me down and being by my side through it all. Every castle needs a queen. I ain't trying to have nobody in that slot if she ain't you. Nah'mean?" I sucked her right sex lip into my mouth and pulled on it.

"Un! Baby!" she ran her hand over her stomach and pulled her other lip apart from the one I was sucking on, exposing to me her pink hole. "You always doing too much, Tristian. Damn, why you always got a start stuff so early in the morning?" She moaned, opening her thick thighs wider.

I know my mother was sweating me, but I had to have some of her. It was early in the morning and I had a wood that wouldn't go down. I had the scent of her on my top lip, and it was driving me crazy. First thing in the morning pussy was the best to me right behind make up sex. I got between her legs, took my big dick head and stuffed it inside of her, arching my back and pounding her kitty out. It was soaking wet, skeeting out of her like baby oil.

She climbed up my body and wrapped her thighs around my waist, and her arms around my neck.

"Oooh, Daddy. Hit this pussy. Hit this pussy hard."
She humped into me, licking all over my neck.

My mother started to beat on the door with anger.
"Tristian! I know you and that lil' girl ain't in there
fucking!" *Doom, doom, doom.* More pounding on the
door. "Get yo' ass out that pussy and down them
stairs, boy! Now!"

I was in the push-up position dicking Perjah's ass
down. Her pussy sucked at me. Her walls milked my
pipe, and sent tingles through my body. I sucked all
over her pretty titties and pulled her nipples with my
teeth.

"Huh, huh, huh, huh! Tristian. Yo' mama. Yo'
mama. Yo' mama. Gon' snap. Uh, shit!" She threw
her head back and left her mouth wide open.

I flipped her on to her stomach and pulled her up
so I could hit that thick ass from the back. I slid back
in and grabbed her hips. She reached under herself
and opened her lips wide while I rammed her at full
speed.

"Shit, baby. Daddy gotta cum. I'm so close." She
bounced back on me with her eyes closed. Her
tongue ran all over her lips. "Get it, Daddy. Get this
pussy. It's yours." Her ass cheeks jiggled every time
they crashed into my abs.

I grabbed a handful of her hair and got to fucking
her as hard as I could. I needed to nut. I was so close.

My mother threw open the door to my bedroom
and stood on the side of the bed with her eyes bugged
out of her head. She covered her mouth with her right
hand and looked on as if she was a deer caught in the
headlights. "Oh my God."

Perjah looked over her shoulder at her and tried to push me off of her. Her mouth was wide open with a trace of drool coming out of the corner "Baby. Baby. Stop. Stop. She right there."

I was too close to let anything or anybody detour me. The way I was seeing it, my mother had to have known that we were in there screwing. I was a grown man and it was my mansion. Perjah was my lady, and as long as she was staying with me I was going to hit that pussy whenever I wanted it, and that morning, I wanted it worse than ever. I pulled her back into me so hard that her ass shook along with her breasts. Her nipples stood out from her mounds about an inch. I slammed into her ten hard times, going as deep as I could. Clenched my teeth, and let my seed fly in squirts within her womb. "Uh! Uh! Baby!" I groaned.

My mother waved us off and jogged out of the room, closing the door behind herself. "Hurry up and bring yo' ass downstairs, Tristian."

I came all in Perjah and fell on top of her thick ass, tonguing her down. I sucked all over the back of her sweaty neck before biting into it.

"Un, Tristian. You so bogus. You gon' make yo' mama hate me, Daddy." She raised her back and my dick fell into the crack of her cheeks. She reached behind herself and opened them for me. "Umm, you want some of this?"

My dick throbbed against her ass. A clear gel leaked out of my head. The pole was glistening after being dislodged from her essence. I put the head on the crinkle of her asshole and started to worm my way inside.

"N'all. Daddy, grab that K-Y out of the nightstand and do me before you go downstairs. You got me so hot right now. Come on." She got on her hands and knees, looking back at me, sucking on her bottom lip.

I rushed and grabbed the K-Y, but before I squirted any of it into my hand, I spread her ass cheeks and licked up and down and in between them, sucking on her anus. My tongue slipped in and out of her backdoor. I bit into her cheeks, stood up and dropped a portion of gel right on to her rose bud, and smeared it around with my dick head. "Un!" She was tight. All that ass and I couldn't believe how tight she was.

"Uh! Do it, Daddy. Hurry up before your mother come back up here."

I pushed forward and impaled her on my dick. Grabbed her hips and got to long-stroking that backdoor with my teeth clenched it was so hot, and murky. She spread her knees all the way apart and crashed back into me. Her ass cheeks jiggled. Her toes curled and I watched her pinch her clit and rub in it in short circles.

"Fuck me, Tristian. I'm yours. Hit this ass, baby. It's yours. Oh, Daddy. Daddy! Daddy!" she moaned, slamming back into me harder and harder.

I grabbed her right tit for leverage and my hips were a blur as we did our thing. My dick ran in and out of her asshole, opening and closing it. The scent of sweat, pussy, and ass wafted into the air.

She grabbed the pillow and bit into it, screaming from the back of her throat. Her fingers continued to play between her legs. "Aw shit, I'm cumming, baby.

You fucking my ass so hard. I'm cumming. I'm cumming!" She arched her back and crashed back into me five times real hard.

I grabbed her curly hair, yanked on it as I stabbed forward, and smacked her ass cheek, causing it to shake before I came deep within her bowels. We fell to the bed breathing hard. My chest heaved. There was sweat pouring down my back and along the sides of my face. I rubbed all over Perjah's ass as she laid on her side looking over her shoulder, smiling at me.

* * *

After my shower, I grabbed me a big glass of orange juice and made my way outside on the back patio where my mother was seated nder an umbrella table, sipping on a glass of wine. She was dressed in a tight-fitting Prada dress that clung to her curves. Her thighs were crossed. She was typing something on her iPad.

When she heard the patio doors slide to the side she looked up and saw me. "Well, well, well, how nice of you to jump out of the pussy so you could join me. Don't I just feel special." She rolled her eyes.

I had on a pair of loose fitting Polo white shorts that were creased, a white beater and some Gucci sandals with no socks. There were two gold chains around my neck and a blunt in my right hand. A glass of orange juice in my left. I sat in the deck chair across from her, sat the juice down, leaned across the table and kissed her on both cheeks. "How you doing this morning, mama?"

She shrugged. "I was doing fine until I witnessed you up there killing that little girl." She reached across the table and smacked me against the head. "Why the fuck aren't you using protection? Are you trying to screw yourself over, and me in the process before you're able to get comfortable in your father's seat?"

I got irritated right away. I mean I loved my mother with all of my heart, but I didn't like when anybody put their hands on me, not even her. "Yo, chill, queen. I got this under control. Besides, that's my lil' boo thang up there. Me and shorty gon' be a part of each other for a long time."

My mother shook her head. "Money marries money, honey. Money is something that that girl ain't got." Her long hair blew in the wind.

It had to be about sixty-five or so degrees, but the sun was out, so it wasn't that bad. It was one of the tamer winters that the city had seen in a long time.

My mother got to typing away at her iPad again. "Says here that she's not even worth a single penny. In fact, she owes the government money for student loans. I can't see how this girl will be a benefit to you or our family's structure in any way, so you need to help me to understand that."

I flared my nostrils and took a sip of my orange juice. All of the sudden I began to get a pounding headache. I needed my Percocet. I needed to treat my nose so I could be numb. My collarbone was killing me as well. "Mama, it ain't about the money for me with her. She has a few degrees and we're going to figure out how best to work with them. But for now, we're just getting our footing. It won't be long."

My mother stood up and walked around the table. She grabbed the back of my neck and put her forehead against mine. "Baby, if I hear you say we speaking in regards to her one more time, your bodyguards are going to have to pull my foot from your ass. There is no we when it comes to her. There is only a you and I until we can fully conquer New York. Are you understanding me right now?" She rubbed the side of my face.

I moved her hand away and shook my head. "N'all, that's my baby in there. That's who I'm about to be with. I love her daughter, and I care about her a great deal. So, when I say we, I'm not just talking about her and me. I'm talking about Brittany as well. They are a part of this family now, and like I said we're figuring things out."

"What about, Kalani? The girl that you've grown up with. The one whom you've helped get through college? What happened to her?" She asked, placing her hand on my shoulder.

"She screwed Juanito, so I can't mess with her on that level no more. Besides, it was over with her for a long time. I'm with Perjah now. Every king needs a queen, and she's mine."

My mother jerked her head back and gave me a look that said she was completely offended. She stepped away from me and paced in her tight Prada dress and red bottoms. Her manicured fingers were on her hips. She'd look at me, shake her head, and then continue to pace, mumbling to herself.

I took a sip from my juice and allowed the cool breeze to wash over me. I still had Perjah's pussy on my mind. I could still smell her in my nostrils. That was my baby right there. I didn't care about nothing my mother was getting at. My mind was made up.

She sighed and sat across from me. "I have you scheduled to meet with some very important people in about three hours. These men own the two aluminum factories that I am looking to acquire on your behalf. The plants will be used to distribute the Vega's heroin and cocaine throughout the United States. As long as you can get it to New York in soda cans from different brands we'll distribute it throughout the country. With Mayor Grant pulling the strings we'll have Carte Blanche. Meaning we'll have the right away to do business as we see fit. From the two plants alone, we'll generate more than ten million dollars a month. We'll use that money to buy properties, and open legitimate businesses. But of course, this is all contingent on you finding a way to use your father's side of the family to get large quantities of the drugs to New York. I am sure that will not be a problem; right?" She picked up her wine glass and sipped out of it. The rays of the sun reflected off of the four three-carat diamonds that decorated her small hands. My mother was a boujee woman. She was the type that had to have the best of the best of everything. She'd been that way ever since my father had come into power. She'd instilled in me, the concept of never settling for less. It was because of her that I had such a deep respect for women.

I swallowed my juice and felt my stomach growl. "I'll make it happen. Ten million a month is good money. Who will be our opposition?" I knew that when it came to the game, anytime you were expecting any form of happiness you had to expect that there was something already in play to prevent that. If my mother was saying we could make ten million dollars a month, that meant that some other drug family would be losing that amount. It was like Pepsi and Coco Cola. No matter how much money Pepsi made they were always trying to find a way to steal the customers of Coco Cola.

She curled her lip. "The Gómezes. But I'm pretty sure that you're very familiar with them. The Gómezes have been a thorn in our family's side ever since your father stepped into power. Bruno has always been a jealous son of a bitch. He's declared war on our family; something about the death of his sons. With you atop the Vega throne, you and I are his number one enemies. He'll be looking to destroy these plants after while. That's if he's not taken care of first." She smiled and sipped out of her glass again.

"Well, you let me worry about getting the dope here to New York, and Bruno. Your job is to do exactly what you're doing. Find opportunistic ventures for the Vegas to cease after exploring, so that we can be as rich as our family is supposed to be. I really am thankful for you mama. I really mean that."

She smiled, stood up, and came around to my side of the table. She moved my arm out of the way and sat on my lap, looking into my light brown eyes. She rubbed my chin with her manicured thumb. "I am the queen, son. Don't you ever forget that. I'ma tell you the something that I told your father when he came into power. All roads must come through me. No matter who you're dating, or fucking, or even marrying; I am the number one queen and you will always honor me as such. To neglect to do will cause you your life. I mean that with every fiber of my being." She leaned in and kissed my lips before standing back up. "Never forget what I just said, son." She waved me off. "Go get yourself together. I'll see you in a few hours. That's if your presence is even needed for this meeting. I have a feeling that it won't be."

I watched her walk along the swimming pool with her hair blowing in the wind. Her dress was so tight that she could only take short steps at a time. I shook my head and laughed to myself. My mother wasn't to be taken lightly. I'd take heed to her advice and never forget her warnings as my father obviously hadn't.

Chapter 6

Later that afternoon, I watched Perjah turn around in a circle as she looked at herself in the full-length mirror. This was the sixth Gucci dress that she'd tried on. Everyone made her look more bad than the last one. She looked over her shoulder into the mirror at her rounded ass. The dress was so tight that I could make out her thong underneath it.

"Yo, word is bond, that's you right there. Gucci need to hire you to be one of their models. Ain't that right, princess?"

Brittany had her wheelchair parked next to me. Her head was laying on my shoulder. "Yeah, mom, you look real good in that dress. Just like a model."

Perjah smiled and smoothed out the material. "Thank you, sweetheart. That makes me feel good." She pulled the price tag from the side of it, and her eyes got bucked. She covered her mouth.

I kissed Brittany on the forehead, before getting up and sliding behind Perjah. I kissed her neck. Her scent was of vanilla. "I know you ain't looked at price tags."

She nodded. "Baby, they want three thousand for this dress alone. You're already getting me the other six. That's crazy. I don't know if I deserve all of this."

I kissed the back of her neck and placed my chin in the crux. "You're a diamond, baby. I gotta make sure that you know that, every single day for the rest of my life. That's all I'm doing."

She looked into my eyes through the mirror and bit into her bottom lip. It was a sexy habit of hers that drove me nuts. She also had this lil' tooth that stood just outside her lower row of teeth in the back. You could barely notice it unless you really looked. But I did often. She considered it one of her imperfections, but for me it was one of the things that I found most sexy about her. "Baby, I appreciate everything that you're doing. It's just so new and different for me. I'm not used to anybody trying to do for me or my daughter. But ever since you came into the picture, you've been like our knight in shining armor. I don't know what to say or do at times. Honest."

I held her and licked all over her neck. "Well, you continue to be by my side, and remain there against all odds. That way I can know I have my Queen and there is no need to look any further."

She turned around no face me. Both of her nipples were poking through the fabric of the dress. "I thought that went without saying. I'd have to be crazy to let a good man like you get away from me. My daughter loves you, and I'm falling in love with you. What more is there to consider, other than our safety, and when I look around, it seems like we're good there." She eyed the five Cuban security men that my uncle Javier had hired to follow and protect me.

You could tell that they were from the island by the snake skinned boots that they wore, their tight Wrangler jeans and cowboy exteriors. All five were armed and dangerous men. They spoke very little English and were down to die for me at all costs. Since taking over for my father I'd bumped up each one of their pay by ten percent. I felt like the more money a man made, the more secure he became. Us

Cubans were big on family. Providing had been instilled in most Cuban men by the time they were seven years old. I felt that my father was paying them just enough to get by. I wanted them to flourish.

"I told you, baby. I got this. I'm a make sure that you and our lil' one are taken care of at all times. I can't lie and say I ain't falling for you too, even though I feel like I'm a few notches ahead." I smiled.

Perjah popped back on her legs and rubbed her ass in my lap slickly enough so Brittany couldn't see her. The dress had been swallowed by her cheeks. "I'm here, baby, and I'm riding with you until the end. I just want you to know that for me it's bigger than the things you provide me and my daughter. I'm falling in love with your heart and the man it belongs to."

I kissed her cheek and held her for a moment, looking into her pretty brown eyes in the mirror.

The bell to Saks Fifth Ave sounded. I looked over my shoulder to see Kalani and two of her friends out of Brooklyn beside her. She had one of the Birkin bags that I'd bought her for her birthday on her arm. She was dressed in a red and blue Burberry dress skirt with black red bottoms. Around her neck was a gold herring bone with white diamonds going through it. She lowered her Burberry shades to the bridge of her nose and scrunched her face. "Oh, hell n'all. I know that ain't my nigga over there."

Her friends looked in our direction. They frowned and looked Perjah up and down. The atmosphere seemed to become sort of eerie.

Kalani pushed her glasses back up on her nose and started to make her way toward us when one of my big bodyguards stepped in her path and prevented her from stepping into our section.

Prior to our shopping adventure I'd paid the manager a thousand dollars to make sure that my security detail could perform their duties. I'd told her that I didn't want to be bothered or accosted. That I was a very important person and would be spending more than $25,000 in their store before it was all said and done. So, as my security guard blocked her path, the manager of Saks turned her back and acted as if she didn't see what was going on.

Kalani took a step back and looked him up and down. "Excuse you?"

He shook his head and held up his hand. "You can't pass. My boss is shopping with his family. They'll be done soon."

Kalani looked like all of her life had been sucked out of her. "Family? You got to be out of your muthafucking mind. That ain't his family. I'm his family. Tristian, you better tell this big ass Cuban Cowboy to get the fuck out of my face before I mace his ass." She took the mace out of her Birkin bag and shook it up.

Perjah stepped away from me and looked up to me. "Baby, who is that?" she asked in her soft voice.

"That's my ex, Kalani. Let me go over there and holler at her before she causes a scene. Here. Use this card and get whatever else you want. It's all on me because I appreciate you." I kissed her lips and leaned down to Brittany. "Baby, listen to me. That woman is my old girlfriend. She's jealous of me and your mother's relationship. I'm going to leave here so I can talk some sense into her. I'm not going with her because I like her. I like your mother, and I love you. Do you understand me?"

She nodded. "Yes, Tristian. I do. But can you not be gone for a long, long time, because I'll miss you. Plus, there is something that I want to show you."

I nodded and rubbed the side of her small face. She was a spitting image of her mother. All the way down to the light freckles that covered her pretty face. I kissed her forehead, holding my lips against her skin for a spell. "I got you, ma." I stepped away from them and up to my bodyguard that was blocking Kalani's way. I spoke to him in Spanish. "I'm going to go down to the truck so I can talk to her. You and somebody else follow me. The other three stays here and keep an eye on my family. Give the order." I stepped past him and grabbed Kalani's wrist.

"Oww, you hurting me. Slow down, where are you taking me?" She asked, stumbling beside me.

Her girlfriends made a move to follow us when they were stopped by my guards.

We wound up sitting in my Range Rover Sport. Me in the driver's seat and her in the passenger's seat with tears in her eyes. "Do you have any idea how it made me feel to hear that man call that broad and her kid your family, Tristian? I feel like I've been gut punched." She cried.

"Kalani, I'm not about to do this shit with you, shorty. You already know what it is. That's who I'm fucking with now; you gotta get over it. Nah'mean?" I let my seat back and turned up the Carters' *Ape Sh*t* and nodded.

Kalani wiped tears from her cheeks. "You gon' hold this one fucking mistake against me for the rest of my life. After all we've been through, you just gone kick me to the curb? Really, Tristian?" She frowned. Her light caramel face was turning red.

"Shorty, I ain't giving up on you. I just ain't fucking with you on that level no more; that's it. Me and Perjah vibing. I'm feeling her being alongside me. I got mad love for her lil' one, and this is just where I'm at right now. I wish you all the best."

I had a bodyguard walking around the truck, and the one from inside of the store that I'd been talking to was sitting in the back of the Range Rover. Growing up I'd seen my pops do the same thing. We were supposed to go on about our lives and say some of the most personal and secretive things regarding our family with a bodyguard standing no more than ten feet away from us. It was crazy but it something I had to get used to.

Kalani faced me and clenched her teeth. "You're my fucking man, Tristian. You belong to me. Nigga, I'd rather put a bullet in your big ass head than to let you move into some readymade ass family. That's my word. While you were running around with that bitch, did anybody tell you that I was pregnant by yo' stupid ass? Huh?" She reached across the console and pressed on my forehead with her finger.

I grabbed her hand and bent that bitch all the way backward until she hollered out in pain. I had a mind to snap that muthafucka because I had warned her about putting her hands on my face. "What the fuck you mean you pregnant by me? Since when?"

She snatched her hand back and rolled it around. "Oww, you fucking brute. What's your problem?"

I grabbed a handful of her hair and pulled her across the console until she was on one knee. "Bitch, what the fuck you mean you pregnant by me?" I snapped, ready to get all in her lil' ass.

"Oww, okay. I've been pregnant for two months. I wanted to tell you, but I didn't know how you'd take it. I didn't think you'd believe me. Let my hair go, Tristian, damn. I ain't trying to be fighting with you." She whimpered.

I reluctantly released it and nudged her head away from me. "Kalani, I swear to God, you bet not be running this weak ass game on me just so I can start fucking with you again. If that's the case, on my mother I'ma put my foot up ya' ass and wear you as a Timb. I know how you Brooklyn bitches get down."

She sucked her teeth and mugged me. "Fuck you, nigga. Now I'm all kinds of bitches and shit, right? You fucking this other bitch, and now I'm just another one of them shiesty Brooklyn hoes that lock niggas down with babies. Tristian, I swear to God, if I was a nigga I'd be beating your ass right now. I don't give a fuck how many guards you got around yo' simple ass."

I swear I didn't like putting my hands on a female. My mother had always told me that some women needed to get their ass whooped in order to keep them in line, while other women, you could whoop them with your words and it would cause just as much damage. Kalani was one of those females that I had to get rough with and communicate by violence. I'd never caused her any serious injuries, but I had gotten into her ass before. On this particular day I had to.

I grabbed her lil' ass by the throat and choked her against the passenger's door for a full thirty seconds while she gagged. I didn't give a fuck. That slick ass mouth was often too much for me to endure without getting up with her glamour. She beat at my hands and kicked her feet in the air. Her Burberry dress wound up around her waist, exposing the fact that she wasn't wearing panties. There were light hairs growing back on her pussy lips. Every time she kicked out at me it exposed more and more of her sex.

"Bitch, are you lying to me? Are you pregnant? Tell the truth?" I growled, choking her for another five seconds and letting her go.

As soon as my hands left her neck, she lunged at me with swinging Fists, fucking me up. I caught a bunch of hits to my forehead, cheeks, and eye. "'Muthafucka! How dare you! How dare you treat me like this, Tristian." She swung harder and harder, making contact.

I allowed for her to connect on more time to my jaw before I smacked her so hard that she fell under the glove compartment with her legs wide open. "Calm yo' lil' ass down!" Blood ran out of my nose and over my lips. I opened my mouth and swallowed it.

My security guard handed me a handkerchief. I used it to tilt my head backward and soak up some of my blood.

Kalani climbed back into the passenger's seat, breathing heavily. She touched the corner of her mouth with her tongue. "Yes, I'm pregnant, Tristian. I wouldn't lie to you about no shit like that. Now I need you to be in my life, but I ain't accepting you fucking with no other bitches. You already know what it is. I get that you and that girl's daughter have a connection, but you had one with me first. I've been there since day one. I know all of your secrets, and I've held you down like no other. You belong with me."

I lowered my head and shook it. "We had a plan, Kalani. You were on the pill. What the fuck happened to that?" I didn't want to be a father to her child. I mean I cared about her and everything and if it came down to me actually being the father, our kid would be straight beyond all measures. But I was kind of over Kalani. I really cared about Perjah. I saw more of my wife in Perjah than I had any female that had ever crossed my path. On top of that, Kalani had fucked my brother. I didn't think I could ever let that go. I ain't think no nigga wanted their brother to know what their woman's pussy felt like. How she moaned and got down behind closed doors was supposed to be special, and a gift only for the man the female was with; at least that's how I felt. Every time I looked at Kalani now I saw images of Showbiz on top of her doing his thing. I couldn't honor that shit. Not now, not ever.

"I was on the pill, Tristian, but life had become so hectic that I didn't always remember to take it on time. Sometimes I'd go a full two weeks. You didn't help matters any by pushing me so hard toward success. Then you was always fucking this pussy. Damn, it damn sure ain't one-sided. Nigga, please."

She pursed her lips and crossed her arms in front of her chest. "So, what you gon' do, because your bitch on her way over here with that lil' girl." She looked out of the window and shook her head. "At least she fine. Some niggas replace their ex with a ugly bitch."

I watched Perjah push Brittany's wheelchair being followed by my security team. Even from afar I could see how beautiful this woman was. I smiled at the way the sun reflected off of her sexy brown skin. There was nothing more special than a beautiful Black Queen to me. In my opinion our race of women were second to none. Perjah was the definition of that.

"Kalani, you already know I'ma be there. I got you. But I want a DNA test to make sure that this baby is actually mine. It ain't nothing personal. I just gotta protect me."

"And who gon' protect me, Tristian? When did life become all about you, and what you got going on?"

"Man, I still love you, girl. But every time I look at you all I see is betrayal. I can't fuck with you like that no more. I can only let a person burn me one time."

She ran her tongue along the inside of her jaw before sucking her teeth. "Aiight, that's how you wanna do shit, right? Okay. I get it." She opened the passenger's door. "On my mother, you gon' reap what you sow if you don't take care of me and mines. I ain't make this fucking baby on my own. I need you, and you better find it within yourself to be here for me or I got yo' punk ass. Until then, nigga fuck you and this bitch!" She slammed the door so hard that it shattered my window.

I watched her bump into Perjah as she walked past her and Brittany. She looked over her shoulder one time before disappearing into Saks. I placed both of my big hands over my face and exhaled. Every time I tried to move upward in life, there was always something or someone trying to pull me down.

Chapter 7

We acquired both aluminum warehouses two months later. It's cost us a million apiece, along with two red bricked houses out in Queens, New York, but in my opinion, it was all worth it. Shapiro helped me to fill the plant with migrant workers from our native island of Cuba. Majority of them had family back home that worked in the Vega heroin and cocaine fields, so there was a connection there. About two weeks after we obtained the plants, I jumped on a jet along with Shapiro and Javier headed for Havana.

It was only my second time flying on a private jet. The first time had been when I was six years old and my father's father had passed away. I remembered being so joyfully overwhelmed at flying in the Vega's jet. I felt like we were a bunch of superheroes. I could also remember thinking that my father had to be the coolest man in the world in order to have made that happen.

But now I was a man of twenty-two years old. I sat in the soft leather seat with a bottle of Ace of Spades in one hand and a blunt in my mouth, taking deep pulls off it. There was a map of Havana in front of me, and a 5'2", strapped Afro-Cuban beside me crushing up ten Perk thirties on a metal tray for my consumption. I could already taste the dope before I'd even gotten it.

She handed me the tray and took the blunt out of my hand, setting it in the ashtray. She was dressed in a real little Fendi stewardess uniform that was so short that I could make out her pussy lips between her thighs as she stood before me. Her scent was Bulgari.

I tooted up two thick lines of the pills and pulled on my nose. I coughed and took a sip of champagne.

Across from me, Javier tooted four thick lines of cocaine. "Nephew, you're going to love being back on the island. All the family are here waiting to throw you a parade. In Havana you are a true king. You are the bearer of the Vega's name. Chico lives on through you. Long live the Vegas!" He howled and continued to toot his lines.

The Afro-Cuban kneeled her thick ass in front of Shapiro and unzipped his pants. The short skirt rose above her hips and broadcast her chubby ass cheeks. There were light stretch marks across them. She stood up and bent all the way over in my face and spread her legs. I could smell her pussy mixed with perfume. Her lips were dark brown and slightly wrinkled. Her box popped out from between her thighs and looked so enticing. She ran her hand between her legs and played with herself, flashing me her pink.

Shapiro looked over her back and guided his dick into her mouth. "This here beauty is one of the best dick suckers in all of Cuba, Tristian, and she's only seventeen. She's legal on the island."

She spread her pussy lips for me and slipped her middle finger into herself while her head went up and down in Shapiro's lap. I could hear the slurping and it made me feel some type of way.

My uncle stood up and smacked her ass, causing it to jiggle. "There is an island full of these, Tristian, and they're all waiting for you." He pulled one of her ass cheeks away from the other one and ran his fingers up and down her crack.

She moaned and arched her back. "Ay, Papi, give me some of that grown man's dick." She said this Spanish.

Javier started to unbuckle his pants, pulling his dick out. "You ain't gotta tell me twice, sweetheart."

I slipped out of there and headed toward the front of the plane to call up Perjah so we could Facetime each other. When she first appeared on the screen, a big smile came across my face. Damn my baby was so fucking bad. "Hey there, mami? How you doing back home?" I asked, getting comfortable in my chair.

I looked toward the back of the plane. Me and the Afro-Cuban made eye contact. She winked at me and ran her tongue all around her lips.

Perjah shook her head. "I'm doing horrible, baby. I miss you so much already. I wish me and Brittany could have come with." She smiled weakly. "Do you miss me?"

Javier slid into the Afro-Cuban from the back and got to fucking her hard. Shapiro pulled her low-cut tank top over her head and tossed it on the floor of the Jet. Her double D breasts spilled out and clapped against her upper stomach before he grabbed a hold of them and suckled.

My dick had snaked its way out of my Ferragamo pants. It throbbed up against my belly. I squeezed it out of the sight of the camera. "No doubt. I just had to call you so I could see that pretty face of yours. I'm missing you like crazy, lil' one."

"Aww-uh. Daddy, do you have to be down there the entire week? I don't know if I can be away from you for that long, honestly. You got me addicted to you or something."

The Afro-Cuban straddled Javier's lap, reached under herself, and slid down his thick pole rolling her lower waist in a circle. His dick stuffed its way in and out of her pussy. She threw her head back and moaned. Shapiro stood on the side of them stroking his dick up before feeding it to her. There scents slowly made it over to me.

"I'ma try and get back as soon as I can because I miss you too, baby. When I get back, I say we go and spend a night out on the town. Maybe a short cruise or something. How does that sound?" I squeezed my dick again and stroked it. The pills had me feening for some pussy. I was wishing that I had brought Perjah along. I would have had her bent over one of the leather seats already.

The Afro-Cuban screamed at the top of her lungs. "Ay, Papacito, give me this dick. Uh-yes!" She started to bounce up and down on Javier as if he were a horse.

Perjah frowned. "Baby, what was that?"

"Yo, my uncle and lawyer fucking the stewardess and she being all loud and shit, see." I turned the phone so she could see what was going on. I wasn't going to have that kind of relationship with her where I lied or kept a bunch of stuff from her. I respected her more than that. I wanted for us to have a special relationship where it was built on truth.

The Afro-Cuban turned all the way around so that her back was to Javier's chest. I could clearly see his dick going in and out of her pussy now. Juice oozed out of the sides and dripped off of his nut sack.

"You see what I'm saying, baby?"

She swallowed and nodded. "So, what are you planning on doing down there? I guess we never discussed that."

"What do you mean, mami?" I squeezed my pipe and groaned. The Afro-Cuban stood up and Javier's dick dropped out of her hole. It was wide open. Juice ran out of it and down each of her thighs. She bent over the couch, and Shapiro got behind her.

"I mean, are you planning on sleeping with another woman while you're down there? If you are, all I ask is that you use protection. Don't bring me back any diseases or anything like that. Please, Tristian."

I shook my head. "I'd never do you like that, Perjah. I got more respect for you than that."

The Afro-Cuban flicked her tongue at me before running it All over her lips again. She closed her eyes and moaned as Shapiro drove into her juice box from the back, whimpering to himself.

"You never answered my question. Are you planning on sleeping with another female while you're on your native island? If so, can you tell me that right now so I can deal with it emotionally before you get back to me."

"Look, Perjah, I called you because I was missing you. You've been on my mind like crazy. I haven't been to Havana since I was six years old. I don't know what is to be expected over here, but as far as me fucking with another bitch, that ain't on my agenda of things. However, if something like that arises, I will respect your wishes and strap up. You got my word on that."

She frowned, and I noticed her eyes began watery. "Okay, Tristian. Well, I guess I'll talk to you later. Text me when the plane lands so I can know that you made it there safe and sound. I'll miss you, baby. Later."

"I'ma miss you too, boo. Later."

I hung up the phone with mixed emotions. On one hand I felt like I didn't give her the response that she was looking for, but I couldn't bring myself to lie to her. Fucking another female wasn't at the top of my list, but at the same time I already knew how seriously fine the women were back on my island. I mean you had women that were mixed with Black and Puerto Rican, Asian, White, Hawaiian, Spanish, and everything in between. Havana was like a smaller version of Miami. I didn't want to say I wasn't gon' enjoy myself, and then slip up.

I cared about Perjah. In fact, I think it was safe to say that I even loved her. I could see her and I going the distance. She was what I imagined my wife would be. I knew that in time I'd be able to be one hundred percent monogamous to her, but at this time I was only twenty-one, and I was going to Havana, the motherland of the Vegas.

* * *

My family had a big mansion right at the top of Trujillo Way. It had twelve bedrooms and ten baths, was three stories, and had a swimming pool, tennis court, and full basketball court amongst other things. It was tucked away in the woods on a fifty-acre estate. The mansion was white bricked and guarded by twenty armed Cuban assassin's that referred to themselves as The Demons or El Diablos. They were a crew of vicious head hunters that ran under my father. Savages that I had inherited.

I sat in the back of the gold Rolls Royce, puffing on a Cuban cigar stuffed with Havana lime green Kush. I was so high that my eyes were slits. I had seven Percocet in my system, so on top of being high I was numb. I took a sip from the bottle of Ace of Spades as we rolled through the gate of the Vegas mansion.

It had to be about eight o'clock at night. The sun had completely gone down. The Rolls Royce pulled up in front of the red door of the mansion. Two armed guards jogged to the side of the car, looking around before one of them opened the door so I could step out after Javier.

"Welcome, Mr. Vega. Your family is waiting for you inside. I hope that you enjoy your stay, Boss. I'll personally make sure that you are safe and sound." He touched the tip of his hat and stood back.

I stuffed a hundred-dollar bill in his shirt pocket as I stepped out into the night. Big lightning bugs were flying all around in the air. I yawned and stretched my arms over my head.

Javier put his arm around my shoulder and led me up to the door. "I hope you to enjoy yourself, Tristian, but know that before you leave the island you have to get an understanding with the Diablos. Casilias was the one that you were talking to. He's head of them. He's in charge of the fields when we are back in New York. It's important that we up his pay and do something special for his family. What do you say?"

"I say you give me a better understanding of his worth, I'll consider it. How does that sound?"

He slapped his hand on my shoulder. "It sounds like you and your father are just alike." He smiled and opened the door.

I stepped inside of the mansion and the first thing I noted was that it smelled like all types of savory foods. It was also cool on the inside compared to the sweltering Havana night. I felt instant relief. My stomach started to growl. I was about five steps inside when the lights flipped on.

"Surprise!" my family yelled in unison.

I flinched by the sudden noise. My heart was nearly beating faster than an African drummer on steroids.

The room was mostly dominated by the female members of my family. My grandmother was the first one to rush over to me and kiss both cheeks. Along with all the rest of my family, she spoke to me in Spanish. "Ay, baby, look at you. You've gotten so big. You look just like, Chico." She ran her fingers through my hair, and then rubbed my broad chest. "Isn't he just the most handsome man you've ever seen?" She kissed me again and pinched my cheek.

I wrapped my arms around her and gave her a nice hug. My grandmother was a slim woman with big breasts. She was five feet even with light brown eyes like myself. I kissed her on both cheeks and released her. "It's nice to see you too, Grandma. I've missed you so much."

My father's sister, Allie, stepped up to me next and wrapped her arms round my neck. She kissed my cheek and held me for thirty seconds without saying a word. Allie had two strip clubs on the island, and ran a big brothel that tourists spent millions of dollars in a year. She had been an ex-stripper herself, and still maintained her figure. She had green eyes and long, curly black hair. Every time she came to visit in New York when me and my brothers were little kids we'd peek through the keyhole in the bathroom whenever she went to shower, or act as if we had to piss so she'd let us come inside. Then through the shower curtain that was clear and basically see-through, we'd turn into lil' perverts ogling her body. I was ashamed to admit that fact, but it was what it was.

She kissed my cheek. "You're a man now, nephew. You're big and strong. It's so good to see you." She took a step back so the rest of the family could get their hugs and kisses.

I didn't leave in front of the door until I'd hugged and kissed more than twenty women. I felt so loved up that I couldn't help blushing.

After all of the love and affection, I sat down to a table full of Cuban cuisine. There was so much food that I didn't know what to put on my plate first. All of the women were throwing something different on my plate, or into my mouth telling me I just had to try it because they'd cooked the dish. When it was all said and done I was stuffed.

My aunt Arlie had a daughter by the mane of Alisha. Alisha and I were the same age. Whenever Allie came out to New York she'd always bring

Alisha along. Her and I were real tight, and out of my cousins I think I loved her the most because we were mostly alike. Alisha was 5'3" tall, Afro-Cuban, like myself because her father was Black. She caramel complexed, with piercing green eyes like her mother, and a strapped body like her as well. She also had long, curly hair that fell past her waist.

She waited until I was done eating before she pulled me away from the family and into her bedroom and wrapped her arms around my neck before kissing me on the lips. "Damn, cuz, I've missed your ass. I'm letting you know right now that when you go back. I'm going with you." She hugged me again and exhaled loudly.

I laughed and took a step back. My family in Cuba was extremely affectionate. Sometimes it felt a little too affectionate. Alisha was so bad that I couldn't allow for her to be all over me like she was, even though I was a grown man now, and my body would most likely respond to her a whole lot different.

"Why you looking to leave the island? What happened?" I asked siting on the edge of her bed.

She sat beside me and laid her head on my shoulder. "I'm just tired of being here. There is always something ridiculous going on. On top of that, things are very intense with the Gomez family. Everywhere either of us Vegas go, we have to be on high alert, worrying about their impending attack. Did you and Juanito actually kill Wisin and Chulo?"

I shook my head. "N'all. Well, at least I know I didn't. Why are the Gómezes so sure that the brothers are even dead? Has their bodies turned up some place? Do they have actual footage of us killing them? I don't think so."

Alisha shrugged. "To be honest with you, I don't care. I just want to get the hell out of here. The other day, on my way home from the salon, Pablo Gomez threw me up against my car and choked me until I blacked out. I woke, there was spit in my face. I'm pretty sure that he did it. My bodyguards were dragging their asses, and because of that, my mother fired them. They crossed over and work for the Gómezes now, which sucks because they have a lot of our family's security intel. Javier is saying that I shouldn't worry, but what's to do when the Gómezes are hobnobbing with the Castros which is one of, if not the strongest families on the island? All of those suckers are cruel, too, Tristian. We can never know what they're up to. I just want to be out of here. I have five hundred thousand in cash saved up. I'm thinking of owning my own strip club out in New York and bringing some of the chicks over from the island. The guys back in the States go crazy for mixed chicks like us. Maybe you can back my club just a little bit to help me really take off. And who knows what'll happen. All I know is that I honestly have to get the fuck out of here."

I was listening to everything that she'd said, but the whole situation was fucking with me. I didn't like no man putting his hinds on any of the women in my family. There was nothing that got me more heated than that. I clenched my jaw over and over again. I could feel my blood pressure rising. "Alisha, as long as you're doing something productive, that will also produce wealth for the Vega family as a whole, I'm going to stand behind you and make sure that you are successful at it. I'll give my mother a ring and see if she can find you a building that we can upgrade. Of course, I'll need your business proposal and need to hear a little bit more about your vision. But I got you, mami. You already know what it is."

She squealed, jumped up and wrapped her arms around my neck before kissing my lips again. "Thank you so much, Tristian. I won't let you down. I'll have my proposal ready to go along with a few of the girls willing to travel up there with me. It's time to get off this island and make my own way." She kissed me again and rushed out of the room.

I sat in thought for a second and shook my head. I was still having the thought of getting up with that nigga Pablo.

Javier stepped into the room and stood before me. "Nephew, I want to give you a tour of the Vega fields first thing in the morning. I know you'll be a bit tired so it'd be wise for you to get a little rest. I'll have Alisha escort you to your room."

Alisha stuck her head in the door and waved for me to follow her.

The room that I'd be staying in was huge. There was a big bed middle of it, and a mini refrigerator on the right side stocked with champagne. On top of the dressed was a bowl of Havanna's Lime Green Kush, and a box of Cuban cigars. There was a big window that gave me a view of the island from the hill our mansion as built on. A ceiling fan hung right above the bed. On the wall was a fifty-inch smart screen television. There was a big bathroom connected to it, and over all I felt like the room was fit for a king. I couldn't complain.

I jumped on the bed and kicked my shoes off, lying on my back. I was tired, and my eyes were already threatening to close.

Alisha stood at the foot of the bed with her arms crossed in front of her. "I'm so glad that you're back for a little while, Tristian. I'm going to make sure that you have a really good time before you go back to New York, taking me with you of course." She jumped up in the bed and hugged me.

I put my arm around her and yawned. "That sounds good, mami." Before I could hear her response to that, I was out like a light.

Chapter 8

I had never been so irritating in my life. As I walked through the Vega fields there were so many bugs flying into my face and crawling all over me. It seemed like every time I'd smack one big ass bug, another would land somewhere else on my body. It would either bite me or crawl on a portion of my body that made me itchy. I couldn't for the life of me understand how the workers could come out to the fields every single day and not lose their minds. It definitely made me respect them that much more.

I looked up to Javier and he seemed as if none of it bothered him. That irritated me even more. I was ready to get out of there and back to the mansion. He used a big stick to navigate his way through the plants. "Tristian, this field is the heart and soul of our family, and its wealth. It started out as only five acres of sugarcane. Now, we have three hundred acres and only a quarter of it is sugarcane." He paid no mind to the big fly landing on his face that slid across his forehead. Another landed on his cheek and crawled across it.

Something landed on the back of my neck and went into my shirt. I jumped into the air and shook my shirt. I was itching so bad that I wanted to kill something.

Javier laughed. "Calm down nephew. It's only a bug. Bugs have been a part of our field since the beginning." Not only were the number of bugs ridiculous, but the fields smelled so bad that I was having a hard time breathing. I pinched my nose. "What is that smell?" I asked gagging.

"It's Donkey shit. We use it as a fertilizer. It helps the cocaine and poppy plants to grow more potent. You'll be smelling piss as well. Nothing is more important than the fertilizer you use for these crops, Tristian. Never forget that."

I had bugs crawling all over me. I was super agitated. I'd seen fifty workers plowing away at the fields. Javier had arranged for men on horses to oversee the workers as they picked and bagged the necessary crops. I saw kids as young as five years there. Swear drenched their little backs. Most of the boys worked alongside their fathers while the little girls worked with their mothers. They looked focused as bugs landed all over them. I felt somewhat guilty at the sights. It reminded me of slavery that the Black side of my family had to endure.

"How much are we paying these people, Javier?"

"They get five dollars an hour. The children four. For most of the families it's enough to put a substantial amount of food on their tables and clothes on their backs. It's a good deal."

"And how many hours do they work on average a day?" I saw three little boys about the of six dragging a big bag of cocaine leaves. Sweat dripped off their chins. They were without shirts. Their skin was sun-baked and red. I felt sick to my stomach. I had so many questions.

Javier shrugged. "It depends. On average I say most families work about ten hours a day. Sometimes twelve, depending on their debts and obligations."

I saw a Cuban guard on a horse swing a big stick and whack an elderly woman across her back with it. She fell to her knees and struggled to get up. He jumped off his horse and grabbed a handful of her hair. Before I could think about anything else, I made up the distance between myself and them. As soon as I was about four feet away from him, I took my pistol out and turned it around. He raised his stick, ready to chastise the woman further, but before he could I rushed him and slammed the handle of my gun into the side of his forehead, cracking it open like a big boiled egg.

He staggered backward with his arms out in front of him. He fell on his ass with blood running out of his wound. He touched the side of his head and looked at his fingers.

I kicked him in the chest and held my boot on his neck. "You will not put your hands on these women while you work under me, you son of a bitch. Do you understand?" I yelled to him in Spanish, pressing harder on his neck with my foot.

Javier rushed over to me, along with a few of the bodyguards. "Nephew, what are you doing?" He asked, looking down on the bleeding man. He went to grab me but decided against it after my guard stepped forward and aimed their guns at him, ready to pull their triggers. I had given them the order to do so if it ever looked like I was in danger, to murder on sight with no hesitation.

"This muhfucka think he gon' work in the Vega fields and beat the women. He got another thing coming. My mother's side of the family were slaves and I'm pretty sure they had to endure a bunch of bullies like this. Not on my watch." I turned the gun around and cocked the hammer. "Javier, I want you to call every one of these men on horses over here.

Hurry up! I'm gon' make an example out of this muthafucka right here and now."

Javier took a step back and got on his walkie-talkie, speaking in Spanish to call for the riding men to meet him at our location.

The older Cuban sister slowly made her way to her feet. Hunched over, she stumbled into me and fell to her knees. "Oh, please, Mr. Vega, don't hurt him. The backlash for my family will be too much to bear. I only wish to do my job, but my back keeps going out. I'll work harder; I swear." She cried, holding her hands together in prayer position.

Ten men riding their horses came and stopped, circling me. The man beneath my boot groaned. I kept my foot on his neck with no mercy.

"How old are you, ma'am?"

She squeezed her eyelids and tears ran down her cheeks. "I'm sixty years old. I have no one to help with my bills. My husband died two years ago and son was murdered by the Gomez regime last summer. It's just me. I'm forced to make a living. I don't want any trouble."

I was really pissed because this woman could've been my grandmother, mother or any vulnerable woman in world. That frustrated me. I took my boot off of his throat. "Why were you beating her?" I hollered.

He sat up and coughed. "She's lazy. There is no need for her here. She's always behind and can't handle her load. She got what she deserved. She's only a slave. What respect do I owe her?" he spat.

Boom. Boom. Boom. Boom. My bullets slammed into his body and caused him to hop up and down on the dirt. The shells from my bullets resonated all around me.

"Listen. From here on out, any man caught beating one of these women will lose their life! I won't tolerate it on any level. You are not bigger than they are. All of you fall under the Vegas. Do I make myself clear?" I asked, looking around at them.

They nodded in unison before I waved them off and back to their places.

I helped the older woman to stand, bent over and dusted off her pants and shirt. Then I took the handkerchief out of my pocket and wiped her face free of sweat. "Listen to me, queen. From here on out I will make sure you're given the best health care and that all of your bills are paid indefinitely."

She shook her head. "No, no, no, Mr. Vega. I could never ask you to do something like that. Working here is enough for me."

I held her face in my hands. "It's done. I will have it all arranged." I kissed her forehead and did everything for her that I'd promised. I made sure that she never had to work another day in her life. Every month she received a $5,000 deposit in her account. All of her bills were paid by the Vegas and they would continue to be whether I was dead or alive.

* * *

Two days later, it was hot and storming on the island. I'd spent the whole morning at a meeting with the ambassador of Cuba where me and Shapiro negotiated the cost of tariffs that would be slapped on our heroin and cocaine as we moved it off of the island. The Castros were looking for something in the range of a million dollars for every ton moved. Instead of arguing about that one, I decided to give them the one-point-five so that all parties could agree. I knew that with my mother obtaining the two factories and using the mayor of New York's leverage to navigate the Big Apple and his political connections abroad, we were looking to make no less than thirty to forty million a month. We needed for customs and the authorities in Cuba to be on board with our endeavor. There were a lot of palms to be greased and I was looking to get as dirty as possible because the long-term payout would be amazing.

Shapiro stepped into my father's old study in the mansion, sipping a glass of orange juice. He was followed by Javier and one of my bodyguards. I was sitting behind my father's desk, looking over an e-mail and a bunch of pictures that were sent to me about property all over Brooklyn and the Bronx. He said that it would be beneficial for us to move in on it because in a short period of time it would be worth three times what we paid for it. I had to agree.

They sat across from me. Shapiro handed me a laptop already opened. I looked at the screen and saw that it was an account in the Cayman Islands. The balance was $25-million. I frowned and looked over at him. "What's this about, Shapiro?"

He smiled. "This is what you have to work with, among other things. Your father said that whichever son took over the business that this money would be for them to strengthen the family. So, this money is yours to do whatever with you please. I'd suggest that you use it to invest in stocks, bonds and real estate. All of the things that will appreciate in value."

He stood and turned the laptop so he could type on it. "Unfortunately, it's been brought to my attention that your father owes the Russians." He turned the laptop back around.

There was a red balance of $15-million. "What's this?" My eyes damn near popped out of my head. "Russians? Why is this the first time I'm hearing about some shit like this? What kind of business did we have with them?"

"Your father was into foreign trade real heavy. The Russians longed for the Vegas cocaine. Before your father passed away, they sent him fifteen million. He placed twenty-five in this account and another twenty. There was no way that he could face you and admit to such a thing."

This was why he was really looking forward to breaking into the Red Hook Houses in Brooklyn. Not only are they the drug capital of America, but if we were able to obtain them, they'd gross a million a day. That's $30-million a month. Not to mention that we were thinking of taking over a few other spots in New York before we ventured out all over the United States.

I slammed my hand down on the desk. "But I just walked around a big fucking field of product. You're making it seem like the Vegas are broke. Explain to me what you're saying!" I snapped at them both.

Shapiro shook his head. "The Vegas aren't broke, Tristian. Calm down. What we're saying is that there isn't much money as there should be. You're going to have to do some investigating and conquering and in no particular order. The Vegas are solely dependent upon you."

"And the reason for this meeting?"

Javier looked up at me. "You've been quite generous with the workers by upping their pay and making sure that all of are happy working under you. While that's cool, I'm not sure we're going to be able to sustain the financial obligations for an extended period of time. That's if we don't move fast."

I nodded. "Any suggestions? Is there anything that I can do before I leave for New York?"

Javier shook his head. "Honestly, here on the island, no one knows about our money issues. Not even the women of the family. I say we keep it that way. The minute it comes out that the Vegas are strapped for cash, we'll be pounced on by a bunch of rival families looking to wipe us off the map. Our best bet is to come up with a plan to take over the buildings as your father intended. We're in no position to pass up a million dollars a day."

"He's right, Tristian. We need to start there and work our way around the city. Investments are extremely important at this point."

"There is one more thing, unfortunately," Javier spoke up. He ran his hands through his wavy hair.

"This just keeps getting better. What's that, Javier?"

"Kosov—the Russian billionaire drug lord that your father is indebted to wants to have a sit down with you first thing in the morning. He's already in Havana at the Bellagio. He says he wants to meet and that he won't take no for an answer. He says the fate of the Vegas depends on your decision."

"That sounds more like bully, Tough Tony shit right there. He think we supposed to be scared or something?" I snapped with sweat on my forehead. I didn't give a fuck who this Russian muhfucka was. I wasn't about to let my family fold to nobody. I'd rather he kill all of us in cold blood first.

Shapiro sighed. "I think you should meet with him, Boss. It's too premature within your reign to be warring with two powerful enemies at the same time. We still have the Gómezes to worry about. Kosov is ten times more powerful and more connected than them. There is no harm in the meeting. At least then you'll be able to see where he's coming from."

My head was spinning. There was so much coming at me at one time. I had to make the right decision, not just for myself but for the Vegas all over the world. I wished my old man had told me about half of this shit. I didn't know the first thing about dealing with a fucking Russian. I mean, I'd watched Training Day like everybody else and saw how they got down in that movie. But could that be real?

I sat back in my father's chair and ran my hand over my face. "Aight, Shapiro, set up the meeting. Let's get this shit over with so I can see what's on Kosov's mind. I got a lot of shit to figure out." I sat back in my seat, mildly angry at my father. How could he leave such a debt? How could he leave the family in such turmoil? I was having some crazy thoughts in regards to my father.

Chapter 9

The next morning, I woke up to Alisha kissing my cheeks. "Get up, Tristian. There is somebody that I want you to meet." She cooed, kissing me on the lips and rubbing all over my stomach muscles.

I opened my eyes and stretched my hands above my head. She slowly came into focus. She was dressed in a sheer light blue nightie. I could see her nakedness underneath. She sat back on her hunches and looked over her shoulder. There was a blue-eyed, dark golden colored female who looked like she stood about 5'7". She had long, curly hair that fell below her shoulders. Her lips were painted red. She was dressed in a red, see-through negligee. Her dark brown nipples poked through the material. She climbed on the bed and grabbed a hold of my pipe, squeezing it in her small hand.

I had chosen to fall asleep without boxers. The silk sheets felt good against my naked skin. "Yo, what y'all on, ma?"

The Cuba girl pulled my skin back and sucked all over the head, twirling her tongue around it before deep-throating me.

I made a move to get up, but Alisha pushed me back down on the bed. "Yo, you good, Tristian. Just let my girl hit you off. She's a beast at what she do. She eat pussy just as good too." She put two fingers into her panties and started moving them in and out of her box with an open mouth. She kept her eyes pinned on what her friend was doing to my dick. Then she lowered the straps of her gown, exposing her perky D cup breasts.

The Cuban moved her fist up and down my pipe. She slurped me into her mouth and moaned around the head. Alisha took her negligee off and smacked her on the ass before pulling her head up, exposing her nakedness.

The Cuban girl moaned with her head thrown backward. "Ay, finger me, Alisha. Do me like you did me last night. Please." She looked back at Alisha, then popped me back into her mouth.

Alisha bent her over, kissing along her spine while she played between her own legs.

I had to close my eyes. Her pussy was right there in my face. It was bald and open. The Cuban chick wasn't making it no better with all the sucking she was doing. Alisha pulled her up by the hair and they got to tonguing each other down before sucking on each other's nipples. My dick was throbbing harder than ever. I had to climb out of the bed or I would be seconds away from doing some shit that I knew I'd regret. I started to slide out of the bed when the chick grabbed me by the dick and held on to it.

"No. Where are you going? I want you to fuck us, Mr. Vega."

"Yeah, Tristian. What's goof? Everybody's asleep." Alisha slid two fingers up the Cuban chick's box before sucking them into her mouth.

It was like fate stepped in. My phone started to vibrate on the dresser. I walked over to it with my hard dick in my hand and saw Perjah's name come across the screen. "Yo, raincheck. I gotta take call." I held the phone up so they could see.

Alisha poked her lips out and grabbed the chick to her. She kissed her lips and rubbed all over her ass.

She bent over on all fours, and I watched the Cuban chick slide her fingers in between Alisha's thick lips, into her hole. Alisha closed her eyes and moaned, sucking on her bottom lip.

I squeezed my dick and walked into the bathroom, pumping it. I sat on the toilet's lid so I could see what was going on but created enough distance so that Perjah couldn't hear their moans. "Yo, what's good, ma? I'm missing you right now."

"I'm missing you too, baby. I just wanted to call you to let you know that. It's been lonely without you here for the last few days."

"We'll I'll be back tomorrow. I need you to hold it down until then. Just know that I'm keeping you at the forefront of my brain and staying focused."

"I was gon' wait until you got back to tell you but guess what.?"

I watched Alisha straddle the Cuban chick. They interlocked their legs and stated to rub their pussies together while the Cuban chick squeezed Alisha's titties and sucked on her nipples. Alisha tongued her down and humped into her from the bed.

"What's that, baby?"

"Brittany moved the toes on her right foot two days ago. Then, today, she moved the toes on her left foot. We're at the doctor's office now. Baby, I'm so happy. I wish you were here," she cried.

I watched as my dick laid against my navel. "What? Are you serious?" I was overjoyed and couldn't wait to get back to New York, so I could see my princess. I was hating that I missed her first few twitches. I felt I had somehow failed her. I needed to get off the island. I missed my lil' family.

"Baby, you do. Just hurry up and get back to us. It don't feel right being beside her without you anymore, and you have no idea how hard it was for me to admit that."

"Well, I appreciate it, am. Tell my princess that I love her. I'll be home soon. That's my word."

"I will. You hurry up."

I sat there on the toilet for about two extra minutes after the call had ended. I was trying to imagine Brittany wiggling her toes, the happiness she must've felt because of it, and then the sadness because I was not there to witness it. I loved her with all my heart. I felt like she was actually my baby. I was missing her and needed to be by her side. For the first time since I'd been on the island I was becoming homesick.

I got up and walked into the room. Alisha was holding her lips open and bumping her clit against the Cuban chick's. They were both moaning at the top of their lungs. It caused my dick to jump but I couldn't allow for myself to succumb to the temptation that was trying to pull me in their direction. I was feening to join them, but instead I grabbed a change of clothes, and went back into the bathroom where I showered and shaved, preparing for the day.

* * *

Four hour later, I settled into a big leather chair across from Kosov, the Russian billionaire. I puffed on a Cuban cigar stuffed with Havana Lime. Shapiro stood to one side of me, and Javier was on the other. I had ten of my Cuban armed bodyguards in the room, ready for war. Kosov had the same number of killers.

He opened an envelope full of the Vega's cocaine, and poured it out onto a golden platter. He picked up a straw after making six thick lines, tooting away two of them right away. He pulled on his nose and coughed.

"So, Mr. Kosov, what brings you to Havana? This is the land of the Vegas," I said, puffing from my cigar.

He laughed and nodded. "The Vegas owe me fifty million dollars plus interest. I'm glad that you came for the sit down. I had other things in mind." He rubbed his nose then picked up the bottle of champagne.

"It was just brought to my attention the deal that you made with my father. I'm sure we can work something out. That way there's no bad blood between us."

He shrugged. "There is nothing to work out. You owe me fifty million plus interest. I come for my money, or we have to have other talks. It's as simple as that." Kosov was very muscular with a blonde buzz cut. He looked like he was fresh from the military. He was dressed in an all-white Armani suit with the matching shoes. He wore a Rolex watch on his left wrist and an ear piece in his ear. His eyes were blue and piercing.

I laughed and puffed off of my blunt. "Well, unfortunately I don' have that kind of money just yet, but I will. I am willing to pay you a stipend each month until the fifty million is recovered. I have a few business interests that are looking to payoff real soon. Patience on your behalf would be more than appreciated.

"Under usual circumstances patience wouldn't be a problem but your father has already received more patience than I am willing to extend to any man. I need my money as soon as possible or I'm afraid there will be bad blood between us. I mean, I don't want it to happen, but sometimes that's the way it goes." He curled his lip and tooted a thick line of cocaine.

My temper was getting hotter and hotter. I felt like he was trying g to stall on me or something. I wasn't with that shit. There were so many things that I wanted to say, but none of them would have diffused the situation one bit.

Shapiro leaned into my ear. "Ask him if he has any solution in mind. Maybe there is something that he wants that we have." He stood back up and briefly placed his hand on my shoulder.

"Kosov, seeing as I don't have the fifty million at this juncture, maybe there is something that the Vegas have that you'd be willing to negotiate for?"

Kosov smiled and took a sip of his champagne. "Of course, there is always something in mind. Take for instance this cocaine that you have here. It's pretty good. Leaves me numb in all the right places and lifted in others." He pulled his nose with his thumb and forefinger.

"Maybe can get you a couple of kilos on the house until I'm able to cure this situation. It won't take me long. I can assure you that."

He broke into a fit of laughter. "Oh, no. You're not dealing with a fucking crack dealer on the streets.

You can keep your kilos to yourself. What I'm talking about is the field. I want fifty percent of the Vega's field until I'm paid with the fifty million and ten percent interest."

"Fifty percent? Are you out of your fucking mind? And with this, what are you are you expecting to do? If it's sell our product, then you're sadly mistaken."

Kosov sat his glass on the table and wiped his mouth his hand. "Not only do I intend on receiving my money in full, but I'll also continue with operations on my behalf of the Vegas as I see fit. The sooner you get my money, the sooner I will ship out. That's how it's going to go. It's the only way you can avoid a war. That will be devastating for you namesake."

Javier frowned and lowered his eyelids into slits. "Mr. Kosov, you make a lot of threats. It appears to me that you see my people as weak, with no backbone. Is this your assessment?"

Kosov waved him off. "I don't talk to the help. You're either the head of the family or nothing more than a glorified security guard. Filter your questions through this one right here." He pointed at me with his head. He had a distasteful look on his face as if he was disgusted by Javier's presence.

I didn't like this Russian. He made my blood boil. I felt my heart thumping in my chest. "Do you have any respect for my family whatsoever? And what makes you think that you can take something that the Vegas have grown through blood, sweat and tears?"

"I don't care about the Vega's blood, sweat, or tears collectively. I only care about my money. If we cannot usher out a deal, then the Vegas will shed much blood. This will cause many tears. That I can promise you."

I looked him in the eye and saw the psycho that lived within. He was a man drunk with power. He seemed to have very little regard for my family. I couldn't understand how my father could become involved with such a man. I saw myself killing him one day. I wanted to take it there with him. I needed to play Chess with this animal. He was clearly richer. More than I was. I was stuck with the burden of finding a way to see all of that against him. It wouldn't be easy, I knew that for a fact.

"Okay, Mr. Kosov, what are the terms of this contract between my family and yourself?"

"You will pay me all of my money before two years pass. If two years pass and I am not paid in full, the one hundred percent of the Vega's fields will be mine. There will be no further negotiations. This is the deal that is on the table. You can it, or we can start this war tonight for all I care. Havana will be left in Shambles. The Vega's blood will flood the cobble streets." He picked up his glass of champagne and took a swallow from it.

I stood up and looked down on to him. This made the entire security detail cock their weapons and raise them just enough to show that they were ready to go.

Kosov's Russian hit men cocked their weapons as well and look from one man unto the next. He simply smiled and tooted another line of the Vega cocaine.

I mugged him with intense hatred. "I don't give a fuck who you think you are, or how much money you have. Ain't nobody gon' spill the blood of my family without paying the ultimate cost. Now, it is clear that you and my father entered some sort of deal that was damaging. I am willing to rectify this, but I will not sit back and allow you to continually disrespect or threaten my bloodline. If it's war you really want, then it's war you'll get." I was fed up with this so-called tough mafucka. How dare he come onto our land and act like he was running shit? This mafucka had come all the way from Russia, and that alone was pissing me off.

Kosov held up his hand. "Say, I hear where you're coming from. Maybe I was a bit out of line. If somebody would have said the things to me that I've said to you, it wouldn't fair well for them. I assure you that war is the last thing I want to bring unto the Vegas. Nobody makes any money during wars other than the manufacturers of the weapons. I only wish to regain my money. As soon as I get it, we'll be off your land. I'm giving you two years. I find that completely reasonable."

I had so much slick shit to spit at him, but something in me told me to hold my tongue. Now that I was the head of my family it was in my best interest to use words for actions. Nah, I had to show and prove. My actions had to come from a strategic place all times. With this situation, my hands were tied. I didn't have any wins going up against this dude. I was forced to submit and surrender over fifty percent of the Vega's fields. It hurt me to do so, but for the long-term success of the family, it had to be done.

***

I felt like I had the stomach flu as I watched the Russians set up shop in our fields early the next morning. I mean, they rolled up in ten Hummers and filed out of them on some military type shit. If it wasn't enough, eight black SUVs were behind the hummer filled with the workers that would do the same jobs that our workers were doing. They set up their troops along the fifty percent border of the field and made them face so that it appeared that they were overlooking our half. They had assault rifles in their hands. They spoke Russian from bullhorns and gave orders of what was to be done.

I felt so sick that I threw up twice as I watched them get things in order. I felt so emasculated. I had to get, Kosov's money and take back my family's fields.

On the night that I was set to fly back to New York, Alisha came and knocked on the door and came into the bedroom that I was staying in. She had two suitcases in her hands with a bright smile on her face.

I was laid on my back with my forearm over my eyes. I was still fuming over the Russians moving in on our family's land. I looked up at her with my head pounding. "What's good with you? Why you got suitcases and shit?"

Her face dropped. "What are you talking about? I'm going with you. You said that when you went back to New York that I could come. Why are you changing things now?" She asked starting to look sick in the face.

I sat all the way up and exhaled. "I'm gon' have to send for you. When I get back there I gotta hit the ground running. It's a lot of shit that I have to accomplish in a short amount of time. There may even be a war breaking out. I can't have you in the middle of that shit."

While everything I was telling her was the truth, I was leaving out the fact that Alisha would have been a major distraction and temptation for me. I know how crazy that might sound, but it's the truth. Not only did she have boundary issues, but she was so fine that she was nearly hard to resist, and I couldn't put myself in that position. Neither Perjah nor I. I had intentions on sending for her when my mother found her a building that her club could be moved into. She would need a place to stay. She definitely could not stay with us. I could only imagine how that would work out.

Even though I appeared to have my head on straight, I was still only twenty-one years old. I was highly sexual, and it was hard to turn down pussy from a bad bitch for me. Because I had so many feelings developing for Perjah, it was becoming a little easier, but I was still going through the process.

Alisha stood up and began to pace the floor with her fists balled up. "You can't leave me in the cold, Tristian. I don't want to live on this fucking island any longer. I feel like I'm losing my mind. I don't care about any war or whatever I'll have to endure in the States. I wanna go. Please. I'll do anything." She dropped in front of me and laid her head on my thigh, looking up at me with her green eyes. She reached between my legs and grabbed my dick, squeezing it.

I grabbed her wrist and stood up. "Yo, see that's what I'm talking about, shorty. If I let you rollout with me, I'ma wind up doing something that I'ma regret, and it's gon' disgrace the family. I gotta see beyond what you're offering. But I do love you. Just give me a few months to get my shit straight, and I'll be at you. I promise."

She bit her lip. She looked me in the eyes. "And this is what it's going to be, huh? You're going to run the same script on me as the rest of the men in our family? Okay, Tristian. It's no biggie. If you won't fly me over to New York with you tonight, I'll find my own way. Just know I'll never forgive you for this. In fact, I hate your fucking guts. You're not the cousin that I remember you to be."

She broke into tears and ran out of the room whimpering. I had the mind to go and chase her, but since I ain't know how that would've gone, I just decided against it.

Chapter 10

As soon as I opened the door to my mansion, dropped the bags on the floor and slammed the door I heard Perjah's feet stomping on the floor, running down to me.

"Tristian! Tristian! Oh my God! Baby, is that you?" She hollered.

I met her at the bottom of the stairs. She jumped into my arms and I twirled her, kissing all over her neck. "Yeah, it's me, baby. How have you been?"

She stepped up to me, kissing all over my lips and neck. "Umm, Daddy. I missed you so much. I been feening for you."

I rubbed all over her ass that were encased in some white lace boy shorts. They were all in her crease. I missed that ass. I squeezed it and gripped the cheeks while my teeth dug into her neck. "Daddy missed you too, baby. Where is my Princess?"

I mean, I wanted to lay Perjah down, but at the same time I needed to see Brittany. Ever since I had found out that she was able to wiggle her toes I had not been able to stop thinking about her. I felt so guilty for not being there when the big moment occurred.

Perjah rubbed all over my chest and looked into my eyes. "Don't be mad, baby, but she's with her grandparents. They've been asking to see her for almost a month. I figured with you coming back after being gone for nearly eight days that you'd want to spend a little time with me so we could, you know, catch up." She smiled, then bit my bottom lip.

I can't front. I was a little jealous that Brittany was away with her grandparents. I thought that she'd been just as excited to see me as I was her. I guess I had to chop it up and be happy for her fine ass mother standing in my face, ready for me to pound her lil' thick ass out. I needed some relief anyway.

I sucked her lips into my mouth and picked her up. She wrapped her legs around my waist and moaned into my mouth.

"It's good, Boo, I need some of this anyway."

Somehow, someway, we made it upstairs to the master bedroom. Perjah ripped my shirt off of me and I stepped out of my pants. Next came my boxers. My dick sprung out like a brown garden snake with multiple veins all over it. The crabapple head pulsated. It pressed up against her stomach as I ripped her blouse off of her, and then her bra. Both breasts spilled out into the open. I picked her up and threw her backward on the bed, pulled her panties off of her thick thighs, exposing her kitty. The lips looked extra puffy. I could tell she was excited and ready for me to do my thing to it, and I couldn't wait to oblige.

She opened her thick thighs wide with the bottoms of her feet on the bed. "Did you miss this kitty, Daddy? Un-uh. Look at her. She's drooling for you." She took two fingers and opened her brown sex lips, exposing her glossy pink on the inside. Traces of clear gel oozed out of her opening and slid onto her ass cheeks. She pulled her lips upward so I could see her erect clitoris. She pinched it. "Daddy, I want you so bad. Tell me that you were a good boy in Havana." She moaned and sucked on her bottom lip.

I stroked my dick, looking at her. Her pussy was so fat and beautifully crafted. I licked up and down the crease and swallowed the juices that were pouring out of her. Sucked first one, then the other lip into my mouth before flicking her clit with my tongue.

She held her lips apart. "Ooh. Ooh. Tristian. Daddy, answer me." She hissed with her eyes rolling into the back of her head.

I smushed her lips together and sucked on them. Her saltiness was all over my tongue and I was loving it. "Yeah, boo, I was good. I ain't smash shit. That's my word." I slid two fingers into her hole and moved them back and forth, taking them as deep as I possibly could before pulling them out and sucking them into my mouth. My hard dick throbbed against the bed under me. I ground into it, ready to fuck Perjah, but first I needed to taste her pussy. I was obsessed with its flavor.

She pulled my face into her crease and humped into it with her eyes closed. "Yes. Yes. Yes. Baby. Eat me. You earned it. You earned it. Uh-baby!" She laid on her back. Her hips rose and fell from the bed. She squeezed her pretty titties together and pulled on the big nipples.

I attacked her clit like it was my enemy while two of my fingers ran in and out of her at full speed. "Cum for me, Perjah. Cum for me, now! Cum for Daddy!" I nipped at her clit with my teeth, then sucked on it like a nipple.

She started to shake. She screamed and opened her thick thighs wider. "Aww, fuck! Fuck, Tristian!

I'm about to cum! I'm finna cum, baby!" She sounded out of breath. "Aww shit!" She screamed.

My fingers ran in and out of her. I kept nipping with my teeth until she came all over my mouth. I swallowed and swallowed and swallowed. Her juices were all over my lips and chin.

She pushed me on my back, stroked my dick, licking all over the head. "I got you, Boo. I got you." She sucked my head into her mouth and deep throated me like a porn star.

My toes curled. I pumped my hips to go deeper into her throat. I grabbed a handful of her hair and guided her up and down my pipe. She made loud sucking sounds that had me on the verge of cumming before I was ready to. "Fuck. Fuck. Fuck. Perjah. Damn, ma." I clenched my teeth and wrapped her curls into my fingers.

Her tongue ran circles around my helmet. She'd suck hard on the big head, then slide her mouth all the way down it, come up, and nip at it with her teeth, then swallow me again. She was doing it all so fast that I couldn't keep up. My toes scrunched. There were veins all in my neck, and the next thing I knew I was cumming while I reached over her back and rubbed that big booty, playing in her asshole with my middle finger. I shook on the bed violently, cumming real hard.

After she swallowed everything that I spat up, she sucked me back to pull me out of her mouth. "I want you to hit this pussy hard, Daddy. I know you been needing me. I know you want some of this gushy." She teased, climbing on top of me and lowering herself onto my pole while holding it with her left hand.

As soon as I broke through her lips all of the heat from her jewels engulfed me. It felt like I'd entered into a velvet oven with ridges on the sides of it. I placed my big hands on her ass cheeks and gripped them. I pulled her forward aggressively to make her take all of me.

"Huh! Huh! Huh! Yes! Yes! Yes! Yes! My dick! My dick! My dick! Aww! Fuck! Yes! Yes! Daddy!" She arched her back and rode me faster and faster. Her soft lips squished my balls and wet them with her essence. Her breasts wobbled on her chest. The hard nipples rubbed against me.

I trapped one with my lips and pulled on it, licking all around the areolas. They were round and dark brown, the size of fifty cent pieces. "Ride this dick. Ride this dick, Perjah. Ride Daddy. Just like that. Fuck yes!" I forced her into me even harder.

She bounced on me as if she was in a bouncy house. The headboard slammed into the wall again and again. The springs on the bed squeaked. Sweat slid down the side of her face. She sucked her bottom lip and held my shoulders as she rode me, popping her ass as if she were twerking on my dick. "Mine! Mine! Mine! This my dick! This my dick. Oh! I'm cumming, Daddy!" She rode me faster and faster while her walls sucked at me and vibrated.

I squeezed that big ass and held it, bringing her forward to me with aggression. After she came, I slowly pulled out and threw her onto her stomach, pushed her knee to her rib cage, and slid back into her cave of delight. I bit into the back of her neck and growled as I killed that pussy. My pussy. I was stating my claim to that ass right then.

Her cheeks jiggled. She bit into the pillow and dug her nails into the bed. "Tristian. Oh shit. Tristian. Unh!" She backed into me as best she could. "You killing me. You killing me, Daddy." She tilted her face to the ceiling and screamed at the top of her lungs.

My hips were a blur. I was watching my pipe go in and out of her and it was a sight to see. My thick pole stretched her wide. Every time I pulled backward she skeeted juices out of her hole. Her fat ass cheeks jiggled around like Jello. I smacked them real hard and kept on fucking with my seed mounting inside of me. I grabbed her hair and pulled her head back. "I'm 'bout to cum, Perjah. Aw shit. I'm 'bout to cum!" I growled, fucking her so hard that our skins slapped into each other's loudly. I gripped her ass cheeks with my nails and came deep within her pussy, letting my seed fly.

She held her ass cheek apart from the other one, exposing her anus. The crinkle winked at me before I slid my tongue into it, after I'd pulled out of her. "You want some of that ass too, Daddy? Huh? You know you can't fuck me without hitting this big booty too. So, come on. I'm ready." She climbed to her knees and laid her face on the bed, holding her cheeks apart, looking back at me with lust in her eyes.

I pinched her clit and it secreted a thick line of juice from the top of her hood. I rubbed it all around my dick head, pinched it again, and then trailed the juices over her backdoor. I wiggled my big head inside of her bowels and sank all the way to her bottom. My balls rested on her pussy lips that were wide open. Her juices oozed out of her center.

"Come on, Tristian. Do me, Daddy. It's yours. It's yours, baby." She spread her cheeks further apart and rocked back into me.

I slammed forward, pulled back and slammed forward again, hitting that thick ass. I reached under her and took a hold of her swinging breasts. "Give me this ass. Give it to me, ma. This my ass. It's mine. It's mine. I'ma kill this shit." I grabbed her hips and got to doing my thing like a savage.

She pinched her clit and flicked it over and over again. She held her head backward and screamed, fucking back into me. "Pull my hair, Daddy. Pull on it. It's okay, it's sewn in real good. Fuck yes!"

I did as she asked and murdered that ass. I loved the way it slammed into my stomach. It made me want to kill it even more. When a woman was as thick as Perjah, you couldn't play when you fucked her. You had to kill that shit, and that's what I was trying to do because it was so tight and good.

* * *

After we finished, we wound up in the kitchen eating big ass bowls of Cookie Crisp cereal. I was on my second bowl and was still hungry. I looked over at a naked Perjah and shook my head. "Yo, my word is bond, Perjah. You're bad, ma. I can't see myself ever getting tired of that body."

She batted her lashes and laughed. "Well, thank you. But I hope you see more than that. I have a lot more to offer you than just my body." She spooned some cereal into her mouth.

I nodded. "Nah, I'm not saying it like that. I just needed to let it be known that you were killing shit. For a second there, when I was back on the island, I thought I was missing something. There were a few instances where I almost slipped up, and I thought I was gon' regret not doing my thing, but I didn't. When I got back here, you reminded me that wasn't none of them bitches on your level. That's all I'm saying. That's big for me because usually I'd smash anything that was nine or better." I got to eating my cereal again.

"Well, that makes me feel good. To be honest with you, I thought that you were going to sleep with somebody else. I mean we've only been a part of one another for a few months. You are a man, and I can tell that women be all over you, so I figured why wouldn't you have. You really don't owe me anything at this point. We're just dating, right?"

I shook my head. "Hell n'all. I don't really know what you're seeing or what you think this is but I ain't playing about you or Brittany. I want you for my woman. I care about you, and I see myself being with you for a long time. Like I said before, every king needs a queen. Within any foundation a queen will always be the strongest piece. You are my queen. I'm taking you and giving you that title. I don't care how soon it is within our relationship." I pushed the bowl away from me. "Bring yo' ass here." I ordered.

She sat her spoon on the side of her bowl and walked around the counter until she was standing in front of me, looking up at me. She was so short yet just the right height. She came right to my bottom lip. She wrapped her arms around my neck and continued to look into my eyes. "So, you taking me, huh? You just gon' make me your queen, then. What if I had another man that I was dealing with before you? Say we had feelings for each other, and I didn't tell you about him just yet. What would you do?"

"Yo, on my word, any nigga that you love outside of me, I'm killing. I ain't playing either. I don't want no nigga sniffing around my queen. That's just how it's gon' be. You need anything in life I'll take care of that. The same goes for Brittany. I'm not honoring no nigga being around either one of y'all. You got that?" I held her by the shoulders and looked into her eyes. I was serious. I'd made my mind up in that split second after imagining her having another nigga outside of me. I wasn't going. Not my Perjah. It was what it was.

She nodded, peering into my gaze. "Okay, Daddy, but if I'm yours then you're mine as well. Anything that you expect of me when I'm in those streets, with the exception of your work, I'll expect the same from you. It's only fair."

"So, you saying that I can't fuck with no other females, period. I can't even settle for the head of a bitch?"

"I'm saying that whatever you expect from me, as a man, you should be willing to relay the same terms to me." She sucked on her bottom lip. "I ain't saying that we can't have any fun though. I mean, if you want to play around with another woman, as long as I'm there and we're safe, then we can do whatever.

But in my heart, I feel like we should enjoy each other for a little while before we get into all of that."

I wrapped her into my arms and kissed her forehead. "I got you, boo. I won't forget that are human either. It ain't gon' be easy. We just gotta keep it fresh and exciting. As long as we're riding together, I can't see how anything or anyone can come in between us. Nah'mean?"

She stepped on her tippy toes and sucked on my bottom lip again. "I'm riding with you until the end, Tristian. You're saying that I'm your queen, then I want to be just that. You have to place me within a position so that I can wear my crown with pride. No queen should be dependent on a man. I should elevate and accommodate you, and not solely pull you down. Do you get what I'm saying here?"

I nodded. "Yeah, Boo, and I'ma get you right. All you gotta do is let me know what you're trying to venture off into and I'll support you in any way that I can, until my last breath."

She smiled. "That sounds great, baby. I'll do that. The first thing I think you should do before we go any further is get an understanding with this Kalani chick. She came by about ten times while you were gone. She says that she's pregnant with your kid, and she's not going to let you dog her. I wanted to ask you about that, but I figured you'd tell me on your own time. There is no pressure. All I want to know is if the kid is yours or not?"

I sighed and blew air out of my jaws. "I don't know, baby. I mean, she and I were screwing around. We didn't always use protection. I can't say for certain, but either way I'ma find out. Like I told you before, she crossed me by sleeping with my brother, so it ain't no telling."

Perjah nodded. "I get it. But I'ma need you to get your affairs in order. I trust you." She hugged me and walked back around to pick up her bowl of cereal, looking at me from the other side of the counter.

* * *

Later that night, Brittany's grandparents dropped her off. I didn't wait for their car to be out of my long driveway before I pulled her out and twirled her around in the air. She clung to my neck and buried her face in it. When I got her inside of the house, I sat her on the couch and took her sandals off of her feet.

"Baby, show me how much you can wiggle your toes now."

She held the arm of the couch and the placed her right hand on the cushion on the side of her. "Okay. It's getting easier now. At first it was hard." She clenched her teeth and closed her eyes. Very slowly, the toes on her right foot began to move. Then she was wiggling them more and more. She held her left foot out and did the same thing. "See. Can you see it?"

My throat had a big lump in it. I held her ankles up to my sight. My eyes were watery, and I was so happy for her. "Yes, I see it, baby. I'm so happy. It's only going to be a matter of time now. I knew you would overcome it. You're a true warrior." I kissed both of her feet and hugged her little body inside my big arms, picking her up off of the couch, carrying her all over the mansion with me.

For the next week, I spent all of my time with them. I guessed I was yearning for that sense of family over here in New York. I had a hell of a plate in front of me, and I felt like Perjah and Brittany were my only sense of normalcy. When I was around them I felt loved and appreciated. I felt like I had a purpose more than being just a drug lord or leader of my family. I felt good. I knew that ultimately that with them is where I wanted to be. So, I took pleasure in our times together.

Chapter 11

I didn't run into Showbiz until three months later. I'd taken six $6-million of the $25-million out of my Cayman Island account and wired it to Kosov. I'd gotten word from back home that the Russians were grinding in the Vega fields. They were producing a half ton of cocaine a week and shipping it back home to Moscow. I didn't know where it ended up after there, but I was sure they were making a huge profit at our family's expense. It took three months for me and Javier to get the aluminum plants up and running. I'd been a few days away from having a ton of cocaine, and the same amount of heroin delivered when I ran across Showbiz.

Me and Perjah were just stepping out of my 2019 Lexus truck, on our way into Macy's, when Showbiz pulled alongside me in an all red Rafe with the top dropped. He made the pipe roar and turned down his music. Kalani sat in the passenger's seat with her belly poking out of her Fendi top.

My bodyguards surrounded me as Showbiz parked and jumped out of his whip with his curly hair blowing in the wind. It was about seventy degrees outside and windy. We were in downtown New York, on Fifth Ave. I'd had it on my mind to take Perjah shopping for a few items of clothing. I felt her wardrobe needed a lil' touch up. Not only that, but I just like spoiling her lil' fine ass. She was a good woman and it was imperative for me to let her know that in as many ways as I possibly could.

I sort of pushed Perjah into the door of Macy's when I saw Showbiz get a little closer to us. "Gon' in there, baby. I'll be inside in a minute."

"But Daddy, why aren't you coming right now?" She asked as two of my bodyguards stood on each side of her.

"Just go, ma. I'll explain everything in a minute."

"What's the matter, Tristian? You trying to keep that lil' fine thang all to yourself. Damn! Look at all that ass. Shorty strapped." Showbiz balled his fist and held it under his mouth. My bodyguards stopped him from coming more than twenty feet close to me. "Whoa, whoa, whoa. What's this all about?"

I curled her my lip and made my way in his direction. "What's good, bruh? You got something on your mind?"

He laughed and sucked his teeth. "Yo, I need to holler at you, kid, on some serious shit. Tell these old ass Cubans to get the fuck out of my face before I start bucking at they ass."

The sidewalk was already crowded with pedestrians trying to squeeze past us. Horns were being honked in the street, and some people were stopping and recording us with their phones. It was a recipe for disaster.

"What you need to talk to me about, Showbiz? You said everything that you needed to when you put them slugs in my body." I never forgot about what him and my brother did to me. It was in the back of my mind. Sooner or later I was thinking I'd get my revenge. There was just so much other shit on my plate that I had to worry about.

"Son, we need to clap at the Gómezes or it's a wrap not only for me, but for our whole bloodline as well. You need to hear what I got to say to you. Seriously." His eyes were bloodshot red. I was noticing more wrinkles in his face than had been there before. He almost looked sick.

"Yo, where you trying to have this conversation? Maybe we can got to one of these restaurants around here or something."

"Yeah. You can meet me at the Olive Garden over on Fifteenth Street. I got a taste for some lasagna and some of their garlic bread. I'ma say in advance that I ain't on no bullshit either, Tristian. I know you're probably thinking that, but on my mother I ain't."

I looked over his shoulder and Kalani and I made eyes. She looked at me for a few seconds and rolled her eyes before looking off. "Yo, what the deal with you and shorty? That's yo' piece now?" A small part of me wanted to know what it was between them. I mean I still cared about her on many levels. I didn't want there to be any hard feelings between us. On top of that, if they were as close as it seemed then that means that there was a chance that she was carrying his seed and not mine. Call it wishful thinking. I didn't want to be one of those men that had too many baby's mothers. I felt like that screwed up the kids over time and watered down the family structure. That was just my opinion though. I wouldn't have minded having a baby with Perjah, though. I knew it would probably happen sooner or later. But I was simply focused on being the best provider and male role model that I could be for Brittany. She was my heart.

Showbiz looked over his shoulder at Kalani and laughed. "N'all, shorty just wanted to roll around the city in a Rafe, that's all. Yo, I guess I never did apologize for taking her ass down. But you know how it is. It's a chance her baby is mine too. At least that's what she saying."

I felt disrespected and angry. "She told me the same thing." I mugged her over his shoulder. "I hope it's yours and not mine. I don't feel like playing all of them fucking games for the next eighteen years."

Showbiz laughed and shook his head. "I know she lied and told you that we slipped up and fucked one time, but nah. I been hitting that shit for a few years now. Shorty love the kid; what can I say?" He smiled. "I'ma catch you at the Garden in a minute, son. Handle your business and meet me there in two hours." He turned and jogged back to his Rafe as a parking police pulled up behind him with its yellow siren on.

I stepped into Macy's with my bodyguards following close behind me. The revelation about them fucking around for a few years had hit me like a ton of bricks. I felt sick. I started to imagine all of the good times that Kalani and myself had together, and they somehow seemed tainted. When we were together, we fucked damn near every single day. I was trying to figure out where she found the time to give him any pussy. My heart was broken just a tad. I was trying to play that shit off as Perjah stepped into my arms and hugged me tight.

"Baby, what's the matter with you? You look sick as hell. Did your brother just give you some bad news?"

I shook my head. "N'all, it's good, goddess. Let's get you right, then I'ma go handle some business and touch bases with you later on. Brittany should be ready to leave her grandparents' house by that time as well." I placed my arm around her lower back and we commenced to shopping.

* * *

"Yo, I'm talking cutting these niggas' head off, Kid. We gotta make a statement in the most gruesome fashion as possible. It's the only way the Underworld gon' respect our gangstas and the name of our family again. The worst thing that could have happened was for the Gómezes to catch wind that our family is being targeted by the Russians. Now they think it's open season. I say we start to knocking they heads off left and right. Leave a trail of blood in such a way that muthafuckas know it's the Vegas, but they can't really prove that shit. Then we'll be able to take over their operations they got going here in New York and down in Havana. What do you think?" Showbiz asked, grabbing the champagne bottle and turning it up.

I finished chewing my lasagna and swallowed it. I chased it with some grape soda and belched in my hand. "Nigga, the last time I saw you, you was hollering that I'd never be king. You said the only way I'd become king was over your dead body. As I can see, you're still living and breathing, so something ain't right." I sucked my teeth and looking him over closely. "What's really good?"

He forked up a piece of Lasagna and ate it. He chewed hard, swallowed it and chased it with his Moet. "Nigga, if the Vegas aren't in power then what are you the king of? Scratch that. If I allow for the Gómezes, or that bitch ass Kosov to conquer or kill off our bloodline, then it means that my last name has no value. It will forever be tarnished. I was born to be a king, Tristian. Our father's throne was supposed to be placed at my feet, but you took that from me. It's the worst pain I've ever felt too." He looked across the table at me. "I'm forced to work with you because if I don't, you'll lose our bloodline to our opposition. As much as I dislike our old man's decision, I feel like it's still my duty to make sure that this family does not go under. I know you think you're the king, but you're not. A king conquers and never folds. I'm a king, little brother. You're just sitting in my chair."

I drank the rest of my soda and spat the ice cube back into the glass. The restaurant was completely packed. It was so much noise all around me that it was making it hard for me to think. On the one hand I was growing more and more irritated the longer I sat across from Showbiz. The nigga was way too cocky for me. He thought he was the shit and that his shit didn't smell like shit either. Even though he was my brother I had a serious disregard for him. Had he not come out of my Pops' sack I would've had him murdered as soon as he stepped out of the restaurant that night.

"I know that you think you're fit to run this family, Showbiz, and you might be. I mean, who am I to say that you couldn't? But all I know is that Pop left me in charge. He said that I was fit to be king of this family, not you. Ever since the words came out of his mouth, you been acting like a straight lunatic toward me. I thought we were better than that. The fact of the matter is that our blood and family's name is on the line here. We need to unite as brothers and figure out how we're going to clap back and strengthen our home front. Right now, the Russians have secured fifty percent of the Vega's fields. The Gómezes have said publicly that they are out for the Vega's blood. We need to fight under one umbrella toward the common goal of taking back our land and our people. The differences that you and I have against each other can be put on hold until all of this is resolved. Then we can battle it out for the throne. Once there is a throne to protect."

He pulled at the stray hairs that were along his chin. "I agree one hundred percent, lil' bruh. This shit is bigger than us. It always has been. I say we both use our smarts in our own individual ways and make this shit happen. After that, we'll settle our most personal score between each other. But I just want to let you know something." He pulled on his nose and looked both ways for whatever reason. "Even though I was vexed at you, kid, I ain't have nothing to do with the try on your life. That's some shit that Miguel tried to pull off all on his own. I'm a killa nigga. Had I wanted you dead, I'da pulled the lick myself and knocked your brains out of your head, then killed them women in the house. You already know my motto of no stones left unturned, and no witnesses left behind. Word is bond, Dunn."

I nodded. "I don't know what made you tell me that, Showbiz, but I appreciate it. I hope you know I can't take this information and lay down with it. Miguel gotta pay the piper. I can't have this nigga walking around thinking it's sweet. Even though me and you have gotten at each other's chins, I ain't ever tried to slump you. At least not yet anyway." I ran my tongue across my upper row of teeth. I could taste the remnants of the lasagna there. My temper felt like it was boiling over. I saw all kinds of images in my head of me knocking my half-brother Miguel's head off of his shoulders. I was still having a hard time of remembering what had taken place the night I'd been shot up for the second time, but every now and then bits and pieces came back to me. Just thinking about that night while sitting across from, Showbiz had me so heated that my vision was starting to become hazy.

Showbiz shrugged. "If either of you niggas had ever come at me and tried to take my life but failed?" He laughed. "Nigga, I'm letting you know right now that it would be hell to pay the captain. I'm taking off any and everybody that you care about, before ripping your limbs from your body. Y'all already know how I get down. Far as I'm concerned, that fool Miguel made his bed, now he gotta lay in that bitch." He picked up his champagne and turned it up. "Far as these Gómezes go, I got the low down on one of the spots they use to house their workers fresh off the island. The men are about fifteen deep, along with their families. If we really wanna make a splash, we'll murder the whole spot, just to send a message to Gomez himself. Leave that bitch so bloody that if we wanted to we could surf on that shit." He laughed.

I shook my head. "Yo, why we can't catch the niggas away from their bitches and kids? You know I ain't ever been the type to turn my gun on a broad or a shorty. That shit just ain't in me." Ever since I'd been in the game I'd never found a reason to kill a kid or a female. Even when I was along for the ride when Showbiz got down like that, it fucked me up royally. I'd have nightmares for months at a time and feel like their lost souls were sweating me. It was crazy. After most regular kills, I'd only have remorse for about two weeks. After that I was over it. The Cuban horsemen I'd killed in Havana, I'd only had two nightmares over him. After that I was guessing his soul had passed on.

Showbiz shook his head and clenched his jaw. "I don't give a fuck about knocking a bitch nor a kid's head off. A murder is a murder to me. I love killing. I feel like it's a great solution for any problem. I was born to be a killer, that's how I feel." He pushed his plate of food away from him. "Bruh, if we ain't gon' go hard then we might as well not come at these Gómezes at all. I guarantee you that they not gon' hesitate to kill anyone of the women or kids in our family. Why should I give a fuck about theirs?"

"Because it ain't the bitches out here starting these wars, it's the men. And the shorties don't know what's going on, so how can they be to blame?"

"Bitches pull triggers too, nigga. And after what a muhfucka did to my son, I just don't give a fuck no more. I'll smoke anybody at any time. That's just what it is. When we buss this move, don't even worry

133

about it. I'll smoke the whole crib with no effort. All you gotta do is have my back. Kill whoever you see fit, and we'll take it from there. You be throwing me with the amount of love you have in your heart though. I don't know where that shit come from."

I ain't feel like explaining my thought process to him. Showbiz had a cold heart. That was all there was to it. I had my own set of morals and beliefs and I wasn't about to let nobody change them. It wasn't sweet with me. I ain't have no problem killing, it just had to make sense to me. Once you took a life, that life was added to your soul. And when you crossed over you'd have to answer for that to the man upstairs. At least that's what I strongly believed.

"So, when do you wanna do this shit?" I asked, looking around at the crowded restaurant. It was getting so loud in there that I could barely hear the words coming out of his mouth.

"Give me a few months to set shit up. I got these Blood niggas out of Harlem that's fucking with me the long way. Posted a few bails, opened a few traps, and now I got my niggas eating. Let 'em burp for a few months, and in the meantime I'ma set shit in motion so we can cut these Gomez's off at the knees. You keep getting money so our financial standing can increase, and I'll do the same. I'll stay in touch. Just be ready when I call you a few days in advance." He stood up and we shook up and hugged.

Even though I embraced my brother, I didn't one hundred percent trust him like that. I knew I had to do a lot of pondering in the time that we were separated. I was still king, so I had to think like one. The Gómezes had to be annihilated. There was no question about that. Now I just had to figure out what was the best way to dismantle them.

Chapter 12

Once the Vega's plants were fully operational, we filled them with migrant workers from off of the island and went hard. After Javier helped to arrange for a ton of heroin and a ton of the Vega's cocaine delivered, it was packed into aluminum cans for distribution. We used a lot of famous logos to put over our cans to disguise them as a regular Pepsi product. Once the dope was placed into the aluminum cans, they were cased in twenty-fours and sat upon different semi-trucks to be delivered all over the United States.

Majority of the cocaine was sent further up north toward Canada while we sold majority of our heroin to the southern states. The aluminum cans were best to use because in the event that one of our trucks were pulled over and a drug sniffing dog was sent through the back of it, the animal was unable to sniff the work through the aluminum cans. It was genius and had been all my idea.

We'd sell the work just like usual, by weight. Depending on the order sometimes I'd have a full case of the Vega's heroin or cocaine sent to one place. Twenty-four cans of cocaine was equivalent to $500,000. Twenty-four cans of heroin was a cool million. I wasn't dealing to or fucking with anybody that was ordering less than $500,000 worth at a time. I was behind with the Russians and I had to get my family out of debt. We went from making $1-million dollars a week to $3-million a week in less than a month's time. Out of the three I sent two to the Russians and kept on doing my thing. I felt like I was their bitch for the most part, but my objective was to get Kosov paid off and off our land.

My mother bought out two beauty salons and a massage therapy parlor and said that since she didn't see Perjah going anywhere any time soon that she was going to give them to her as long as she allowed for her to keep forty-nine percent stake in each place until Perjah was able to pay her back the money for each place. Personally, I wanted to give my woman the bread up front, but she declined and said she wanted to do it on her own. That my mother was throwing her a bone and igniting a fire under her that needed to be lit. After much discussions I agreed and stepped to the side. They finalized their arrangement and in less than three weeks, Perjah had filled the shop with a bunch of her girls out of Harlem. Them sistas came in with money on their minds and got shit cracking like ASAP.

Perjah was cool enough to extend a hand to the employees that had been working at the places before my mother had bought them out. She hired six of them and kept the manager of the two beauty salons on staff. She was getting her own money, and I was cool with that. Even though she really didn't have to work because I had her no matter what, the fact that she wanted to was enough to let me know that she was my one, and I needed to make it official.

So, Saturday morning I woke up with love on my mind. I'd been trying to come up with a raw ass way to propose to her, and I had so many thoughts going through my mind of how to outdo myself, that I started to second guess everything. So instead of driving myself crazy, I was just gon' keep it simple and wake her up by proposing. I'd already arranged for a 2020 pink and black Range Rover truck to be delivered first thing that morning. The sound of the workers unloading it from the back of their truck is what woke me up this morning. I had them put a white velvet bow on top of it, and underneath the bow was a lil' piece I'd written up from the bottom of my heart. I couldn't wait to see the smile on her face when she got that far. I copped her a three carat, white diamond engagement ring with the gold setting. The setting had diamonds the color of pink lemonade all around it. It had cost me damn near sixty gees, but she was worth it. I had plans on going even harder for the wedding ring. I just wanted to make her happy and let her know that she was appreciated.

So, this morning, I snuck out of the bed after kissing her on the forehead, slipped my boxers and white beater back on, and was on my way downstairs when the sight of Brittany in the hallway freaked me out. I froze in place and felt my heart pounding in my chest like a bass drum.

She was holding herself up with the wall but walking toward the master bedroom with tears running down her cheeks. "Tristian, I can feel my legs. They work again. Look. Can you see what I'm doing?" She cried with a smile on her face.

I rushed to her side and placed her arm around my neck. One of my arms went around her lower back. "Come on, princess, I got you. Daddy got you, lil' mama. Perjah! Wake up, baby!" I guided Brittany down the hallway toward our room.

She took a deep breath and put one foot in front of the other. She'd get a few paces and look up at me with tears of joy. "I'm doing it, Tristian. I'm really doing it."

"Perjah, baby, wake up! Hurry up!"

The next thing I heard was the sound of the headboard and then the springs. She appeared in the doorway of the master bedroom and rushed to our side.

I continued to guide Brittany step by step. She leaned against me. I couldn't help kissing her soft cheek. "You got this, baby. You got this. I believe in you." I slowly eased her out of my embrace. "Go ahead. You got it, mama."

"I know, but I'm scared," she cried, looking down at Perjah then up to me with tears streaming down her beautiful face.

Perjah stood up and rubbed her back. "You got it, baby. Walk for mama. Walk for mama, baby." She took a step to the side of her.

Brittany stood in the hallway on wobbly legs. She shook and bit into her bottom lip before taking a step on her own. "I got this. I got this. I got this." Her legs continued to wobble.

I walked slowly beside her with a huge lump in my throat. My eyes were watery as hell too. It was like I was seeing my child walk for the first time after the doctors had assured me that she never would have. I felt like picking her up and twirling her around in a circle, but I knew that I had to let her finish what she'd started.

She got half way down the hallway, and the wobbling of her legs stopped. Even though she kept a hand on the wall, she looked stronger, more confident. "I got this. I got this. I got this," is all she kept on saying until she made it into my bedroom and dropped to her knees, crying in her hand.

I rushed to her side and wrapped her into my embrace. "Baby, I'm so proud of you. I knew you could do it. I never doubted you." I hugged her tightly and rubbed her back.

Perjah kissed all over her face, crying tears of joy swell. "I'm so happy for you, Brittany. We gotta get on our knees and thank God for this miracle and blessing."

And that's just what we did.

* * *

I didn't even wanna take the spotlight away from Brittany after all of that had taken place, but it was almost impossible when my mother showed up out of the blue and got to running her mouth.

"Whose Range Rover is that in the driveway, Tristian? It better be mine." She sat her Hermes bag on the living room table and put a hand on her hip.

I frowned and grabbed Perjah's hand. "Nah, ma, it ain't yours. It's for my lady right here. Come on, lil' one, let me show you something." I grabbed her hand and led her outside the mansion.

The sun was shining bright outside on this day. It had to be about eighty degrees with a gentle breeze. There were a bunch of birds chirping in the tree about twenty yards away from the front door of the mansion.

I pulled Perjah's hand until she was standing in front of the truck with both of her hands covering her mouth. "Oh my God, baby. I can't accept this. You've already done enough."

I opened the driver's door, took the keys from under the seat and tossed them to her. "You're my baby, and I wanna spoil you. This is what it is, so check it out."

Perjah stood frozen for a second, and then walked around the truck with her eyes wide open. She ran her finger along the side of it and tapped her foot at the big wheels with the pink and black rims on them. "This is too much." She opened the passenger's door and stuck her head in, taking a big whiff of the interior with a smile on her face.

I let her check it out on the inside for about five minutes.

Brittany rolled out of the mansion in her wheelchair and parked it beside me. "Dang, mama, you finna be stunting in this. Tristian always spoiling you." She laughed, looking up at me and shielding her eyes from the sun at the same time.

Perjah jumped out of the truck and got ready to run around to me with her arms wide open, when I stopped her by getting down on one knee and pulled the ring out of my shorts pocket. She froze in place, and her eyes became watery. "Tristian, no you're not. No, you are not, baby."

I popped open the box and took her hand and looked into her pretty brown eyes that drove me crazy. "Perjah, it ain't no sense in me beating around the bush. I love you, and I love Brittany with all my heart. I been crazy about you ever since I laid eyes on you. I felt a crazy connection, and something drawing me to you that I couldn't control. All I see is you, and all I need is you in my life, as my Queen. If you'll give me the chance, I'll prove to you that I'll be the best man that I can be to both you and Brittany. I'm willing to give my all, one hundred percent, and with my whole heart. Will you be my wife?"

The sun reflected off of her forehead. Her edges were slightly curled because of the sweat, and in my mind she looked like the baddest woman on the planet. She looked over to Brittany. "What do you think, baby?"

Brittany wheeled her chair over to Perjah and nodded with a smile. "Do it, mama. He really loves you, and I love him. Why shouldn't we be a happy family?"

The sunlight dances off of the diamonds of the ring. They sparkled bright. Perjah looked down on me and nodded. "I love you, Tristian. There is no doubt about that. I know that you're the man for me and my daughter. All I ask is that you don't change up. Please continue to be this man. Continue to love us unconditionally. I'll be all that I can be to you as well. Until my last breath. Hell yeah, I'll marry you. Give me my ring." She held out her fingers and wiggled them.

I slid the engagement ring onto her left hand and felt my heart thumping in my chest. I couldn't believe that I had actually gone through with it. I was on my way to being Perjah's husband. I was sure that I was ready, despite my age. I came up from my knee and we tongued each other down while Brittany made all kinds of childish noises to indicate that we were in love. I found it cute, and so did Perjah.

My mother stepped out of the mansion and grabbed me by the wrist. "I need to talk to you, mister. Right now!" She snapped, pulling me like I was a kid or something. We wound up in the pool house out back. She walked in the small kitchen, grabbed a plate and threw it against the wall. "Are you out of your fucking mind, Tristian?"

I looked her up and down and tried to calm myself by taking a deep breath and shaking my head. "Yo, what's the problem now, ma?" I didn't feel like arguing or debating with her about who I was going to marry. I didn't think it was her place to tell me who I could and couldn't enter holy matrimony with.

"Son, did I not tell you that money marries money?"

"Yeah, ma, you did. So, what about it?"

"So, if you understand that, why are you proposing to this girl? She doesn't have any money, and what she'll gross from the salons and massage parlor isn't enough to constitute as wealth. You should not be marrying her. You're better than this. I want more for you than this, Tristian."

"Ma, I get that you're a lil' protective of me, and that's cool. However, you ain't about to run my life. Now I love that woman out there. She's my heart of hearts. I can see myself being with her for a real long time. I was supposed to put a ring on her finger."

"But she already has a child. She's not financially stable. Her family is mostly on government assistance. There is no benefit here. Love cannot pay the bills. It isn't worth the emotion. You're fucking up. You're twenty-one and engaged. Get a clue."

I scoffed and had to bite my tongue. I'd never disrespected my mother for as long as I'd been alive but I was finding it real hard to not be that way with her this day. I felt like she was judging my woman; taking unnecessary shots at her and Brittany. I felt offended and angry at the same time. The only way I was able to refrain from cursing and snapping was by biting my tongue.

"I'm sorry, Tristian, but I'm going to have to ask you to go back out there and end things with her. I simply cannot stand by and allow for you to make this huge mistake. At the end of the day we're trying to build a dynasty here. She has no part in it." She turned her back on me and got ready to leave.

"Ma, you doing too much."

"Excuse me?" She stopped and looked back at me.

I walked over to her and pulled her back into the pool house, grabbed both of her wrists and looked down and into eyes. "I understand that you feel like now is the time for us to being going hard, and we will. But I'm letting you know that Perjah will be a part of this dynasty as well. I love her, ma. That's my queen right there. Ain't no amount of money gon' ever change that. You gotta let me do me, and stay in your lane, with all due respect. I know you got my best interest at heart, but you gotta let me live my own life. It's the only way I can become what I'm truly meant to become."

She looked up to me and her face softened. "I just don't want you to make any mistakes, baby. You're still my only son and my little man. I have to look out for you. If I don't then who will?" She rubbed the side of my face.

"I get that, but can't you tell that she's a really good girl?"

She nodded. "Honestly, I like her. I can tell that girl loves you, son. It's written all over her face. It's kind of refreshing. I guess I just need to make sure that she's marrying you for all the right reasons. You're a man of clout now, son. You're a target for single women in her position. You're what they would consider a come up. Mama just has her claws out, that's all."

I kissed both of her cheeks, and then her forehead. "It's good. You ain't raised no dummy. Perjah and I will go the distance. I'm certain about that."

What's crazy is that I believed every word coming out my own mouth. I honestly felt that Perjah was supposed to be Missus. I didn't see any flaws in her character. Plus, I was already head over heels for Brittany. I couldn't see Perjah being with some other man and allowing for him to raise Brittany. In my eyes she was my daughter, and I wasn't playing about her or her mother. They were my lil' family, and I was gon' protect and love them with all that I was as.

Chapter 13

It seemed like everything was falling into place. By the third month of being in production, we were making $5-million a month of pure profit, and $5-million that had to go back into the business and to the island for the Vega's to remain strong and able to see eye to eye with other drug trafficking families. The Gómezes had yet to attack, but word through the underworld was that they were supposed to be mounting us to do the unthinkable. I didn't have any idea what that meant but I was ready to link up with Showbiz so we could the process rolling first.

Showbiz told me to be patient. That he had some shit in the mix that was going to take another three weeks to complete. He told me to trust him, and then when it was time to strike that we would deliver a knockout blow to the Gómezes I was forced to trust in his word in regards to this, so I just kept on getting money.

I had a few distant family members that were block boys in Spanish Harlem that were out there getting some major paper but needed a consistent plug that would help them flood the Bronx all the way back to Spanish Harlem. It took a few weeks for us to get everything up and running, but after it was, I started to catch three hundred thousand every week from the traps in the Bronx, and the hustlers out in Spanish Harlem provided another two hundred thousand. That was a hundred thousand dollars of pure profit weekly. I couldn't beat that. I sent the funds that I made off of them directly to Kosov. That way all of the other profits could be used on the

Vegas in other ways. I'd paid Kosov about $25-million and had another $5.5-million to go.

* * *

Shapiro woke me up one Sunday morning with a phone call. I was laid up in the bed, spooning with Perjah when my phone got to vibrating like crazy. I picked it up reluctantly and saw his picture pop up. I slid out of the bed and walked the bathroom, yawning with my head pounding.

"What's good, Shapiro? I'm sleepy as hell." I was gone after tooting twelve pills the day before. I needed to treat my nose before I began the day. My body was calling for it.

"I thought you'd might like to know that I was finally able to locate that gift that you wanted. It's here and already tied up. I need to know what you want me to do with it."

A big smile spread across my face. You see, Miguel had gone missing in action for more than three months, and I was unable to sleep regularity after Showbiz had basically told me in so many words that Miguel had been the one to hit me up. I couldn't take that hit on the chin. I didn't give a fuck if he was my brother or not. "Shapiro, I'll be there in an hour. Make sure that nobody unwraps my gift before I get there. I mean that."

"I'll make sure, Boss. I'll see you in a little while." The call ended.

When I came out of the bathroom, Perjah was sitting on the edge of the bed with her head lowered. She sucked on her bottom lip and looked up at me. "They found your brother didn't they?"

148

I frowned and stopped mid stride. I was shocked. "Damn, what would make you say that?" I asked, walking over to her and sitting beside her on the bed.

She sighed. "Not only was I able to hear some of your responses to whoever it was on the phone, but I also had a dream that you killed Miguel last night." She yawned and covered her mouth. Her hair was all over her head.

I wrapped my arm around her and pulled her close to me, kissing her soft cheek, then her lips, sliding my tongue between them. I could taste a hint of her morning breath, and I was with that. I loved this woman. I didn't think that I'd honestly say I cared for a woman deeply unless I was able to make out with her first thing in the morning. Most times I got up before Perjah just so I could tongue her ass down.

I was infatuated by her on so many levels. I couldn't even believe that I was man enough to admit that. "To answer your question, you're right. One of my men got Miguel's ass wrapped and waiting on me. I got to get over there so I can make him pay for his sins. I can't honor what he did, nor can I let it go." I made an attempt to rise from the bed.

She grabbed me by the wife beater and pulled me back down. "Baby, why can't you just let this go? I mean, he hasn't messed with us ever since then. You're still alive, and we must let bygones be bygones. Turn over a new leaf. If we want God to forgive us of our sins, then we have to forgive in the others the same right."

I shook my head and bounced off of the bed. "N'all, fuck that, ma. Son put that steel to me. He could have killed me and left me in front of my own crib. Now you already know what it is. I gotta get up with his glamour or else he gon' think it's sweet."

Perjah stood up with her hands out in front of her. "Okay, baby. I get what you're saying, but can you just calm down and listen to me for a second? You know I'll never tell you nothing wrong."

I stepped into my Ferragamo denims, pulled them up and added the belt. I grabbed my bulletproof vest off of the dresser and started to put it on as well. "Perjah, please don't do this, baby. This will be a crazy way to start our engagement." I slid into my black top and put on my holsters, adding a .45 in each one.

She stepped over to me and placed her manicured nails on chest. "Baby, it's my job to steer you away from things when I can. I am more than just some chick that you gave a ring to. I think my purpose in your life is bigger than what we previously imagined. What if I'm supposed to lead you out of the life?"

"What?" Now I knew she was bugging out of her head. I didn't know what was going on inside of her, but I wasn't feeling the words coming out of her mouth. I had too much more evil shit to do before I could ever think about stepping away from the life. The Vega's legacy depended on me being a savage. I wasn't ready to give all of that up, even though I was crazy about her. "Perjah, this what's gon' happen. I'm about to leave this house, get in my truck, and roll over to where this nigga is. Once I get there, I'ma question him, and in the process finding out what I need to know I'm gon' torture this nigga before I kill him in a bloody fashion. Why? Because he's getting what he deserves. It's an eye for a muthafucking eye. Ain't no nigga gon' put that heat to me without suffering the for their actions. I am a king. That shit can't happen."

"Why are you cursing at me so much? I was only speaking of the things that are on my heart."

"Word is bond, ma, I ain't angry with you. I'm just in my mode right now. That animal within is trying to emerge. Let me get out of here. Come here."

She stepped over to me, I grabbed a handful of her hair, and tongued her ass down. "I love you, Tristian. Please be careful, baby. I'll be at the shop by the time you get done. I'm taking Brittany with me today."

"I love you too. Always, and until the death of me. I'm sending four of my men with you for security."

* * *

Before I stepped into the brownstone where Miguel was being held, I sat in my truck and tooted six pills of Percocet. The high would only last about fifteen minutes, but it was better than nothing. I was up to as many as fifteen pills a day, and I felt that it still wasn't enough. I feared that soon I would have to switch over to something stronger. I always felt some type of way whenever I was around the Vega's heroin. I saw that as being a pitstop on the road of my life. Dope was the only thing that had me calm and floating by. I had so much stuff on my plate to figure out that from time to time I just needed an escape, and pills were the closest to an escape that I could get. They were my oasis.

When I stepped up to the backdoor of the Brownstone, Shapiro opened the door with his eyes bucked and glossy. I could tell that he was high. I didn't know from what, but something was definitely off. "Tristian, how goes it, Boss? He's down stairs in the basement waiting on you." He pulled on the tip of his nose and sniffed loudly.

I shook his hand and brushed past him. I figured I'd found out what habit he'd discovered. Right then I was as high as a kite and I wanted to torture Miguel. I took the flight of stairs all the way into the basement. It was lit by a blue light bulb. Miguel was duct taped to a metal chair by his ankles and wrists. There was a black hood over his head. He was shirtless. His chest heaved as sweat was dripping off of it.

I walked up to him and snatched the hood from his head, then the duct tape that covered his mouth. "Well, well, I finally caught up to yo' bitch ass."

"Come on, Tristian. I ain't did shit to you. Why the fuck you got me down here?" He snapped with anger.

Bam! I smacked him with all of my might across his face, then backhanded him the other way. He spat blood across the wall. "You can ice all that tough ass shit. Nigga, you and I know that you's a bitch! But even bitches can get their hands on guns I see." I held my hand out.

Shapiro handed me some pliers. "Here you go, Boss. For what it's worth, I never liked you anyway, Miguel. You're a fucking racist and a bigot." He spat in his face and stood behind me.

The spit dripped from Miguel's forehead, down his face, and off of his chin. It looked like a green rope of slime. That shit was disgusting.

"Yo, you gon' let this fucking cracker spit in my face like that, son? Word is bond, I'd never let a devil do no shit like that to you."

I laughed and grabbed him by the throat. "Bitch nigga, who shot me? Was it you, or was it Showbiz?"

He scrunched his face. "The kid stay rolling so much that my memory ain't shit no more. I couldn't tell you. That's my word." He sucked his teeth and smirked at me.

"Oh, that's yo' word, huh? Aiight, we'll see what that word turns into in a minute. Hold this fucking peasant!" I ordered two of my bodyguards. "And open his mouth."

"Open my mouth? What the fuck you on, Tristian?" He looked around the basement in a panic.

My men did as they were told. The rough and rugged, Cubans slammed him against the wall while another forced his mouth open.

I stepped into his face. "Before it's all said and done you gon' tell me who shot me. It's gon' get real painful in the process though." I took the pliers and clamped them onto one of his front teeth before pulling downward with all of my strength.

"Aww! Aww! What the fuck? Argh!" Miguel screamed like bitch.

I wiggled the tooth from right to left, pulling and twisting it all around until it slowly came out of his mouth with a squirt of blood behind it.

He struggled against my guards, and they held him tighter. Once the tooth was extracted from his mouth, I dropped it on the floor in front of him. Blood gushed over his lips. He swallowed it and tried with little success to shake his head. "This some bullshit, Tristian. You know I ain't shot you, nigga. Why the fuck you playing these games?" He sounded out of breath. Sweat poured down the side of his face.

"What? So you saying it was Showbiz? Huh? It gotta be one of you niggas. Which one was it? Huh?" I put my hand up to my ear. "I can't hear you, nigga? Speak up. Oh, I see. Maybe you got too many teeth in the way." I clamped the pliers onto another one of his front teeth and yanked on it. I twisted it all the way around and pulled it up, then downward, almost falling to my knees as it extracted from his gums.

"Argh! I can't take this shit. Argh! It's too much." Blood spilled out of the holes in his gums. He sounded like those old people who tried to carry on a conversation without their dentures in their mouths. I felt no remorse from him. Not even he started crying like a child. "Tristian, keep them fucking pliers away from me. Please, bruh. Showbiz shot you. I was with him, but he shot you. I wanted to, but my gun jammed. Once he dumped you twice, he ran back to the car. I was supposed to finish you, but my gun was jammed. I was glad, bruh. I swear I couldn't do it." He spat and blood hung to his bottom lip.

I could only speak through violence at this point because I didn't know who to believe. I punched him two quick times in the stomach and ended the combination with an uppercut. His head snapped backward into the brick wall and busted open. I grabbed him by the throat and called Showbiz's line. He picked up on the second ring.

I didn't wait for him to say a word. "This fuck nigga said it was you, kid. I got him in a sticky situation right now. Tell him what you told me, fuck nigga!" I spat at Miguel. "Who shot the kid?"

"Showbiz, come get this crazy ass nigga! He pulling out my fucking teeth!" Miguel hollered toward the phone. I slapped him across the face and punched him in the stomach with my left hand while I held the phone in my right. He doubled over and started to dry heave with blood leaking out of his nose. He took big, heavy and ragged breaths. "I ain't shoot you, Tristian, damn!"

"Nigga, tell Showbiz what you just told me or I'm finishing you, son, word is bond." I put the phone to his mouth. "Tell him, bitch nigga!"

Miguel started to wheeze loudly. His chest heaved. I could tell that he was struggling to breathe. I think I might have broken one of his ribs or something. I wasn't sure, but I didn't give a fuck if I had. He put his bloody face against the phone, closed his eyes and swallowed. "Showbiz, don't let me take this L, kid. Yo, you know my gun jammed. I didn't put no slugs in him. You did."

I wiped the phone on my shirt and clicked it on the speaker phone so I could hear what Showbiz was saying to him. I was starting to believe Miguel. That didn't mean that I wasn't going to buss his ass though. He'd said over and over again that his gun had jammed. In order for you to find out that your gun was jammed you had to pull on the trigger. That meant that he was pulling on the trigger. Had his gun not jammed, his intent was to kill me. I couldn't live with that. He had to pay for his sins one way or the other. I didn't give a fuck if he was my brother or not. He wasn't family; you feel me?

"You bitch made ass nigga. That's why I always said that you couldn't have been Pops' son. You got too much bitch in you to be from our DNA. You gon' tell this nigga that I shot him, Dunn? Yo, word is bond. If he don't kill you, I am. In fact, I'm about to go slice open yo' pregnant bitch right now. The last thing we need is another you in this family. Rest in peace, snake ass nigga. You ain't no blood of mine." The phone call ended.

I was heated. I mean, in so many words I could have surmised that Showbiz was actually behind the pulling of the trigger, but then again he'd never admitted to anything. For a second I was stuck between a rock and a hard place. I didn't know which way to turn or what to do.

Miguel spat a bloody loogey on the floor. He took a deep breath. "You ain't right, Tristian. You will pick a beef with me but don't do shit to that nigga Juanito. I think it's 'cause you scared of him or something. You just prey on the weak. That's what cowards do." He closed his eyes and winced in pain.

I stepped up to him and grabbed him by the jaw with my right hand. "Fuck you, you soft ass nigga. You always tryin' to wiggle yo' lil' weak ass out of something. Whether you pulled the trigger or not, you intended on killing me. If it wasn't for your gun jamming, maybe you would have. For that alone, I can't let you walk out of here. Now I could have one of these old men from the motherland whack yo' punk ass, but nah. I owe my old man more than that. If I'm gon' kill his son, then I'ma be the one to do it." I handed Shapiro the pliers and cracked my bloody knuckles.

Miguel snorted a bunch of snot into his mouth and spat it directly into my face. It was a big, bloody ass ball of spit that was so thick that it barely slid down my face. I had to wipe it off with the bottom of my shirt. I was so disgusted that I threw up in my mouth and swallowed that shit.

"Fuck you, Tristian! That nigga finna use you and take the throne anyway. Showbiz hate you more than I do, and you already know I can't stand yo' punk ass. You can kill me, muhfucka, it's good. I know I'll be seeing you real soon." He spat again, but this time it missed me.

I slid the phone into my pocket, swung my left and connected with his jaw. Then jabbed him in the nose and hit him with an uppercut before working on his body with blow after blow. I was hitting him so hard that I could feel his bones breaking. I didn't give a fuck. I kept on swinging. I'd hated this fool ever since we were kids. He was a racist Cuban that hated the other half of me. He'd had more Black murders under his belt than any other race. I'd never felt a connection to him on any level, and never trusted him. So, I took out all of my frustrations against him, swinging with all that I had.

The old school Cubans dropped him, and he fell to the ground with his bloody face bouncing off of the concrete. He tried to get up, and I stomped him on the back. Cocked and kicked him straight on the side of the face. He flipped over, and I brought my Timbs down, crushing his nose, stomping him until my sock filled with blood. When it was all said and done, I'd fucked him up so bad that his soul escaped from his body. I had the Cubans chop him into little bitty pieces and toss them into the Hudson. Miguel was no more, and I felt like I did the world and our Vega bloodline a favor.

Chapter 14

Ten more of my cousins moved into the territory of upper Manhattan, right on Nagle and Tenth Ave. They bussed into dope game of Spanish Harlem with a vengeance, selling $500,000 worth of cocaine a day and a million dollars' worth of heroin every thirty-six hours. Slowly but surely the Vega's began to move the competing dope boys out of the area. My cousins fanned out and put a Vega in control of each block, from Nagle all the way over to River Park on Dyckman Street. I was their supplier and made sure that they got the best of the best product. Heroin so potent that they could step on it two and three times and it would still be strong enough to leave the feens nodding on the verge of overdose. The Vega's cocaine was pure white like snow. Because it was coming directly from the fields back home, the quality was no less than ninety-five percent at all times. That meant that a dope boy could take thirty-six ounces of our uncut and turn it into three kilos if he wanted, and the dope heads wouldn't know the difference. The smart dope boys of the Vega's only added eighteen ounces of baking soda, or B-12 to their kilos, and popped them like that. By doing this, they were able to keep their clients happy, and at the same time more than maximize their profits.

It wasn't my job to oversee how they ran their slums. I was strictly the brick man. I wasn't coming into Spanish Harlem unless there were more than a million dollars in cash for me to pick up, and there was never any less than that. The aluminum plants started to really take off when my mother linked up with some of her king pin brothers out in Chicago. They were copping $10-million worth of heroin every month and flooding their city. By long, she found buyers out in Detroit, one in Milwaukee, another in Cleveland and another in Iowa. Off of her buyers alone we were pulling in roughly $40-million a month. The orders were coming so fast that we couldn't fulfill all of them soon enough.

The portion of the Vega field that we had was being stripped to the leaf. I wasn't giving them time to replant, so we harvested more of our crop. I needed to regain the other four fields in order to maintain production.

Kosov flew me out to Los Angeles one Friday afternoon in the spring. He'd sent me a private Jet and allowed for me to bring Javier, Shapiro, and seven of my old school killers. He'd previously said that he wanted to meet face to face so that we could discuss more business, which I didn't understand, because prior to be flying out to Los Angeles I'd paid him all of his money in full. In my mind there was nothing else to talk about, other than the fact that his troops had yet to remove themselves from the Vega's fields.

The meeting was held on the third floor, and in the back of a private room of Nobu. We pulled up in a stretch Mercedes Benz limo, and filed inside of the paparazzi infested restaurant. When I made it upstairs, Kosov greeted me with a handshake. He was dressed in a silk Roberto Cavalli robe and fit. There were remnants of cocaine on his top lip, and nostrils.

He pulled on his nose and ran his tongue across his teeth. "Mr. Vega, what a pleasure to meet you once again. I'm glad you could fly out to Los Angeles, the new home of King James."

There were five Russian beauties sitting on the couch here. I guessed Kosov had been seated. They were buck naked, and as much as I hated to admit it, fine as hell with their different colored eyes and voluptuous bodies. Kosov had six of his armed guards stationed in the room as well.

I shook his hand and released it. "Kosov, you're paid in full, baby. It's time to get your boots off of my land and everything goes back to normal. My father is no longer indebted to you, and neither are the Vega's as a whole." One of the Russian beauties handed me a bottle of champagne. She made an attempt to rub my chest when I caught her wrist and threw it away from me. "Sorry, shorty, I like my women kissed by the sun and rolled in chocolate."

I don't think she understood English at all because she smiled and ran her tongue across her lips.

Kosov instructed me to sit on the couch across from him. There was a long table full of platters of Vega cocaine, bottles of champagne and straws. The sight of the cocaine was enough to get me red hot. This Russian was getting high off of my family's supply when our obligations to him had been fulfilled.

I took a seat on the edge of the sofa. Javier and Shapiro sat on either side of me. My guards mixed into the room. One of the Russian beauties tried to come over and sit on my lap. I pushed her ass off of me and onto the floor. "Yo, I don't fuck with these kinds of hoes. Keep 'em to yourself, Kosov, and tell me why the fuck I am here." I demanded, getting more and more vexed.

Kosov grabbed the white bitch by her hair and flung her across the room. She landed on top of two of the other girls. He said something to them in Russian. They huddled into one of the dimly lit rooms and sat with their knees up their chests on the floor.

He turned to me and flared his nostrils. "I thought we were friends, Mr. Vega. Haven't I been more than understanding to you and your people?" He sat on the couch and crossed his legs.

"Yeah, you were, and I appreciate that. Why am I here?"

He chopped through the Vega cocaine before making two thick lines and tooting them up each nostril. He took a pinch, put it on his tongue and ran it all around his teeth. He sat back on the couch with his arms along the back of it. "I need a favor."

"What is the favor?" I was losing my patience with this cocky son of a hitch. With his buzz cut hair, blue eyes, and arched eye brows.

"I need three more months on your fields. If you can give me three months, I'll give you ten million dollars back, and you'll have my respects on a global scale which could be huge for whenever you decide to think bigger than drugs. I am a connected man in many markets. I can help you to turn your money into taxable dollars. Technology is the pillar of the billionaire. If you will extend your hand for me, I can link you to a few upcoming new gadgets that will make you a billion dollars over a five-year span."

"So now I see why your men haven't left my fields." I sucked my teeth. "Your offer is ten million in three months, when in one month I'll make more than that. It just doesn't seem alluring enough for my eyes. I'm going to have to respectfully decline your offer. I want your men off my property and I'll see you when I see you." I stood up, preparing to leave.

"It doesn't work like that, Mr. Vega!" He snapped. "Now sit your ass down and listen to what I have to say to you." He hissed, leaning forward on the couch.

I stopped and looked at him over my shoulder. "Who the fuck you think you is, Kosov? I don't know what type of families you're used to bullying, but the Vegas will never bow down to yo' punk ass. Now, make the call. Get your motherfucking men off of my land, or word to my mother, it's gon' be some serious problems for you."

He took a sip from his bottle of champagne. "So, I guess this is where I run and hide with my tail tucked between my leg." He laughed. "Please, you're nothing more than some insect under my boot for all I care. If I want to step on you, you will cease to exist. Now, sit down. Do it now!"

"Fuck you! You red faced muthafucka. You got my warning, son. Leave my land, or there will be problems." I signaled for my men to leave the room with me.

"You just made a big mistake, Mr. Vega. I'm not the one you ever want to cross! I did a favor for your family. I asked you for one and you spit in my face!

I will not forget this!" Those were the last words I heard from Kosov before we left Los Angeles.

* * *

Two days later, I woke up to the sounds of Perjah throwing up loudly in the bathroom. I jumped out of the bed and rushed to her side.

Brittany was kneeling beside her, holding her hair with a solemn look on her face. "Tristian, my mother's pregnant. She was scared to tell you."

I frowned and looked down at Perjah. She remained hunched over the toilet. "Baby, is this true?" I asked, getting down so I could rub her back.

She nodded. "Yeah, but I wasn't scared to tell you. I was waiting for the right time. Tristian, I don't want to have this baby out of wedlock. We have to do it the right way. Give this child a fighting chance and be united in holy matrimony before it arrives, just as Jehovah intended. Please don't fight me on this." She started to purge her guts again.

I rubbed her back. "Baby, I'm ready when you're ready. I love you, and you mean the world to me. Maybe you're right. Maybe we should bring this baby into the world under God's grace and care." I kissed her cheek.

She flushed the toilet and sat back on her haunches, wiping her mouth with a damp cloth. "Thank you, baby. Our wedding doesn't have to be all extravagant or anything like that. As long as you're my husband by the end of it is all that matters to me." She wrapped her arms around my neck and closed her eyes.

I held her for a moment. "Baby, I'll let you arrange everything and I'll fit the bill. I got you." I kissed her juicy lips and hugged her closer to my body.

Brittany hugged my waist. "You guys are getting married! I'm so happy! Now you'll really be my dad, Tristian."

I nodded and rubbed her little back. I felt good. I was ready to make it official with my lil' family. Ready to step up to the plate more than I already had. As soon as Perjah was able to make it off the floor, she picked up the phone and began to make arrangements with a smile on her face.

Chapter 15

It had been two weeks since I'd sat down and had the meeting with, Kosov, and the Russians were still in our land down in Havana. I felt that Kosov was ready to go to war over our land, and so was I. The only problem was that if I had to wage war with the Russians and go at them full force while they were set up in the fields, I ran the risk of damaging a lot of the crops, and therefore not being able to fulfill any orders from the mid-western parts of the United states, and those orders were keeping the Vegas afloat. I had to find a way to get Kosov and his people off of our property without ruining our crops. So, three weeks after I sat down with him out in Los Angeles, he decided to meet me at the W hotel in downtown New York.

When he walked through the door of my penthouse suite and extended his hand, this time I neglected to shake it. Instead, I remained seated while Javier led him to the couch away from me. I was doped up on twelve Percocet with my heart beating faster than I ever remembered. My face was numb and my throat was completely dry. There were five of the old school guards behind me, with Shapiro sitting to the left of me.

Kosov had a wicked smile on his face. "Mr. Vega, to what do I owe such an honor?"

Two of his big, beefy looking bodyguards stood behind him with their hands in their jackets. Their eyes scanned the room. I could tell they were on edge.

Javier closed the two doors and walked further into the big suite, standing behind me. I mugged Kosov for a long time. I hated the look of his face. I had visions of melting it away with bullet after bullet. I cursed the day my father had gotten involved with such a crook.

The toilet flushed and Showbiz opened the door to the bathroom and walked into the room, drying his hand on a white towel. "Is this that pretty muthafucka Kosov that I'm hearing so much about?" He walked over to Kosov with his hand extended.

"The first born." Kosov curled his lip and frowned. "I will not shake your hand. You're nothing to me. Your father didn't have enough regard for you to hand you his seat. The look of your face disgusts me." He waved him away and crossed his legs. He was a cocky muthafucka. I could tell that he felt that the world should be kissing his ass on a daily basis. "Why have you summoned me, Mr. Vega?"

Showbiz plopped down on the couch and clenched his jaw off and on. He bounced one foot on its toes and couldn't stay still. I could tell he was heated at the utter disrespect from, Kosov.

"Your people are still on Vega's property. The deal was for me to pay you fifty point five million dollars and our debt would be washed away. I've done my part. Why are you neglecting to send your troops away?"

Kosov sucked his teeth and shook his head. "I've changed my mind. After consulting with the Russian Federation, I decided to completely take over the Vega's field and make them official Russian turf. In exchange, my Federation will pay you a sum of two hundred million US dollars. After this, you will be ordered to evacuate our land immediately."

"You got to be the dumbest white man in the world. What part of any conversation that we've had thus far has led you to believe that I am interested in selling even a piece of our land?" I moved to the edge of the sofa. My palms began to sweat.

"I no longer care what you want, Mr. Vega. You have no say in this matter. The decision had been made for you. The Federation has already claimed that land for its own. It'd be wise for you to step back and let this happen, or else I can't imagine all of the things that are about to take place against your family." He shrugged. "I prefer murder over giving away two hundred million myself. So, we can play it any you want." He growled and leaned across the table.

Showbiz upped two .45s that were already cocked, put both of them to Kosov's forehead and stood up. "You see, I ain't like my muthafucking brother. I don't scare so easily. You sitting here talking all of this tough shit about what you and your people gon' do to me and mine. How about I just leave yo' fucking brains on the table right here and right now, white boy?" He pressed both barrels harder into him.

"Mr. Vega, tell your brother to stand down. This will only make matters worse. I am Kosov Putin. Nobody does this kind of shit to me!" He snapped, hollering through his clenched teeth.

The bodyguards behind Kosov had their guns aimed at Showbiz. My troops had their weapons aimed at his. Javier upped a .9 millimeter off of his waist and aimed it at Kosov. I remained seated.

"Fuck you, Kosov. I ain't telling him shit. Let's see yo' tough ass get out of this one." I sat back on the sofa and smiled.

"Get yo' punk ass on the phone and tell them Russians to get off of our land, or I'm putting two in your head, and we'll take it from there." Showbiz hissed.

Kosov looked up at him and lowered his eyes. "You think if you kill me that you're in the clear? Huh? Is that what you think? Well, let me tell you something, that land is as good as gone already. You're fighting for a lost cause. Once the Russian Federation wants something, they take it. Look at what they've done to your White House. The Vegas aren't as important or as powerful as the Presidency of the United States. You want me to call and tell them to retreat? Well, I'll tell you to kiss my Kremlin ass. You filthy ni—"

Boom! Boom! Showbiz's gun jumped in his hand and sent wo bullets into Kosov's forehead. "Bitch ass cracker."

Kosov flew backward and wound up bloodied against the leather sofa with his eyes wide open. Half of his face had been removed.

Javier shot from a silenced .9 millimeter. His bullets connected with Kosov's guards' heads. They jerked on their feet before falling to the ground. "Are you crazy, Juanito?" He put his pistol back on to his hip and stepped into Showbiz's ace.

"What the fuck are you talking about, Javier?" Showbiz asked, mugging him.

"You've just waged the worst kind of wars. The Vega's didn't need this kind of drama. This one act may have not only cost us our land, but it may be the end of the Vegas as we know it. Fuck!" He looked over to Kosov's bleeding body.

Showbiz stepped away from him and looked down at Kosov. "That white muthafucka wasn't about to give us our fields back. You heard him. He tried to treat us like a bunch of bitches. I ain't with that shit. I sent his punk ass on his way, and I'ma do it to every last one of them Russian bitches if I have to. Shit ain't sweet. So fuck what you talking about."

"That's it. I've had enough of your mouth, Juanito." He grabbed Showbiz by his shirt and punched him in the mouth, knocking him over the table. Showbiz's head hit the side of the couch. Javier jumped over it and pulled him up, punching him again in the nose. He made his head slam into the floor before he pulled out his .9 and pressed it to Showbiz's cheek, cocking the hammer. "Say your prayers, Juanito. It's time that we're rid of this plague that is you." He placed his finger around the trigger ready to buss.

Showbiz blinked repeatedly all dizzy like. He looked into Javier's face and squinted. Blood ran from the back of his head and pooled on the carpet. "Kill me, bitch. If you don't kill me, I'ma kill you." He promised through gasps.

Javier held him down. "That's it." He bit his bottom lip.

Boom. Javier's head jerked forward before he fell off of Showbiz with his brains oozing out of his skull. Showbiz wobbled to his feet and looked down on him, staggering from one foot onto the next. I stood over Javier with a smoking gun. I felt sick to my stomach and wished I'd never had to kill my uncle, but I had no other choice. He had been seconds away from killing my brother. Even though there was bad blood between me and Showbiz, I refused to allow anybody else to take his life. I felt that when it came down to it, I would be the one that sent him to the Reaper. I wasn't letting nobody steal that privilege away from me, not even Javier.

Showbiz raised his foot and stomped Javier in the face, repeatedly.

* * *

Shapiro arranged for the entire crime scent to be cleaned up and the bodies disposed of. About four hours later, I watched Javier's body being tossed piece by piece into the Hudson just as Miguel's body had been.

Showbiz placed his hand on my shoulder and shook his head as we watched from the limo. "Yo, Kid, I know you feeling some type of way about wasting that old nigga, but had you not, he would have killed me, Son. I love you for this. Word is bond, I ain't ever gon' forget that."

I waited until my crew loaded into their trucks before signaling to the limo driver for him to pull off. "You know what, Showbiz? I don't know what the killing of Kosov is going to bring unto our family. Whatever it is, I'm ready to die fighting it because I am a Vega until my last breath. Now, when it comes to Javier, I'm sick over that kill, Dunn. That was Pops' brother. He was a good man. You shouldn't have provoked him the way that you did. But it is what it is, though. We gotta move on and figure this shit out before we become victims of the underworld."

Showbiz turned up his bottle of Hennessy, drinking half of the bottle. He stopped and wiped his mouth. "I love you, kid. I know you don't think I do, but I'm letting you know now that I love you as much as my cold heart will allow. I didn't give a fuck about that old geezer. I didn't give a fuck about that Russian, and had you not taken care of Miguel, I was gon' slump that nigga too. My heart is black. I'm fucked up in the head. All I care about is being king of this family. I'm willing to do whatever it takes. I'm willing to kill anybody that I have to in order to obtain my birth right. That shit eat at me every single day." He turned the bottle back up and swallowed it in big gulps.

I watched him closely. He looked like he'd lost another five pounds. He was still muscular, but there was definitely something off about him. I couldn't quite put my finger on it. "You know what, Showbiz? Maybe I ain't the man for this throne. Maybe it is supposed to be rightfully yours. I mean, I ain't seeing what you're seeing. All I'm seeing is a bunch of problems that can't be handled without falling deeper and deeper into the abyss. I want more than this, kid. I always have."

Showbiz nodded. "Then give it to me, nigga. If you saying that you don't want to be king of our family any longer, then denounce your throne and hand it over to me. I'll show you how to reign supreme as a true Vega, against all odds. That's my word." He sniffed and pulled on his nose. "I'ma need access to everything you got right now though. The factories, the fields and all the money. I'm hip to the off-shore accounts too. I'll let you keep a nice amount, but for the most part I'ma need 'em all. It'll be my right to have as king of the Vegas."

I nodded. "Give me a few days to think about it, and I'll let you know what's good."

He smiled. "Nigga, take a month. It ain't no rush. I gotta be out of town for a minute anyway. I got some important people to meet up with. Them Russians ain't the only heavy hitters in the foreign world. In order to destroy an enemy, the Vegas must align ourselves with the enemies of our enemy. You feel me?" He took another swallow from his bottle.

I didn't give him a response to that. But that night I stayed up into the wee hours of the morning tooting pills one after the next. I couldn't believe I had killed my own uncle. A man that had stood behind me one hundred percent. I shed tears as I rocked back and forth in the den of my mansion, with Biggie rapping in the background. The life was starting to get the better of me. It was to the point where I began to question the purpose of the Vega's throne. To sit upon the throne meant that I would never be able to be happy because there would always be somebody or some family gunning for me and my family. It would never end, and I was already tired of it.

Chapter 16

A week later Showbiz appeared at the front door of my mansion with red eyes and a bottle of Hennessy in his hand. "I fucked up again, Tristian." He took a swallow from the bottle and belched real loudly.

I grabbed him by the shoulder, looking behind me to make sure that neither Brittany or Perjah was anywhere within earshot of our conversation. "What the fuck are you talking about, Showbiz?" I looked him up and down. He smelled of alcohol and must. His long hair that was usually kept nice and neat was unkempt and all over the place. His breath smelled funny as well.

He shook his head. "Yo, I understand why I'm so fucked up now, kid. It's my son. I ain't ever been able to grieve over him, and I had to do what I had to, Tristian. You gotta understand where I'm coming from." He tilted the bottle and started to take a series of gulps from it. I ain't mean to do what I did. Not to her, but I had to. It's the only way I'm gon' be able to grieve, kid." He scratched the inside of his forearm and I could see the needle marks.

"What the fuck are you talking about? You did what to who?"

Perjah came down the stairs in some tight pink boy shorts with the matching pink wife beater. When she saw that I had company she made her way back up the stairs. She stopped at the top, covering her crotch area and her breasts. "Baby, when you have a second can you come up here so I can speak to you?"

I nodded and waved her off. "Yeah, bae, in a minute. Let me see what's the matter with my brother."

"Okay, Daddy, but please, whenever you get the chance. It's important." She disappeared down the hallway.

Showbiz rubber necked, looking up the stairs. I thought he was trying to see my baby's ass and that pissed me off. He grabbed me by the shirt and balled the material into his fist. "I fucked up, Tristian. You gotta forgive me. But if Maine ain't no more, then she shouldn't be either. My son was my everything. I had to avenge him. You gotta see where I'm coming from." He pushed me back and opened the door to my mansion. He stopped and looked me over before stepping out into the daylight.

I squinted, not understanding what he was talking about. I jogged to the door as he drunkenly got into the driver's side of his Rafe. "Showbiz, who the fuck are you talking about?"

He pulled his leg into the car and slammed the door. He started the engine and revved it by stepping on the gas. Then I saw the window roll down. "Tristian, don't hold this shit against me, Boss. Remember, I'm your blood. That's thicker than water." He peeled out of the drive way with the bottle of Hennessy turned up. I watched smoke waft from his tires as he sped away.

I stood there in the hallway scratching my head. "What the fuck is he talking about?" I asked out loud before shaking my head. "That nigga gotta be bugging right now. Word up." I closed the door and made my way upstairs.

Perjah was sitting on the edge of our bed, rocking back and forth with a .45 in her hand. "Is he gone, baby? Did you tell him to leave our home?" she asked with wide eyes.

I frowned and closed the door behind me. I knelt in front of her and took her manicured hands into mine, kissing the backs of them. "Baby, yes, he's gone. You're safe now. Do you hear me?" I sat beside her and pulled her into my embrace.

"He's the devil, Tristian. Every time I see your brother I feel like I'm in hell. He's evil. I've been having lot of bad dreams about him." She blinked tears. "He's going to hurt one of us, baby. I can feel it."

I frowned and held her tighter. "I'd never let nobody hurt you or Brittany. I already told you that. Speaking of which, where is my daughter now?" I asked looking around as if she was in the room.

"She spent a night with her grandparents. She'll be there until Sunday afternoon. Don't you remember me telling you that?"

I shook my head. I couldn't for the life of me remember us having any conversation about Brittany going anywhere. I shrugged and kissed her on the cheek. I could feel her body shaking. "I don't remember you telling me that, but if you're saying that you did then I won't put it past my selective hearing. But I want to talk to her to make sure she's good."

She nodded and stood up. "Let me go and get her grandfather's new number off of the counter. I just wrote it down last night and forgot to add it to my phone. I'll be right back." She stood up and placed the gun on the bed, shivered, and walked out of the room.

My phone began to vibrate on the dresser. I grabbed it and put it to my ear after answering it. "What's good, Shapiro?"

"Boss, have you heard from anybody back in Havana lately?"

"What? N'all. Not since a few days ago, why?"

"Tristian, the Vega's mansion was under heavy fire the last I checked. The fields have been set ablaze. I haven't been able to confirm who the attackers are, but I have reason to believe that it is the Russians. I need to meet with you as soon as possible. There is only one move we can make to squash the beef with Kosov's people. But I won't say it over the phone. I'll be there in an hour. I'm on the jet."

My head was spinning so fast. "Alright, Shapiro, keep me in tune, man. I'll keep trying to get a hold of some family from down there." I hung up with him and called my mother. phone rang and rang, but there was no answer. I sent her a text telling her to get back to me as soon as possible. I spent the next few minutes calling and texting as many of my family members in Havana that I knew. I was unable to receive a response from any of them. I felt like throwing up. The world was spinning so fast.

Perjah walked into the room with her hand over her mouth. She shook her head. "Tristian, not my baby again. Not my baby again, Tristian. Please God, not my baby again." She fell to her knees and dropped the phone she was carrying, screaming into her hands.

I rushed to her side on the floor. "Perjah, what are you talking about? Where is Brittany? What's the matter with you?"

I removed her hands from her face. Before she could open her mouth to say anything, there were tires screeching to a stop in front of the mansion. I heard multiple doors opening and the sounds of boots on the gravel before the shooting started. *Boom-boom-boom! Boom-boom-boom! Boom-boom-boom!* Our attackers began to chop at the mansion.

Perjah covered her ears and screamed at the top of her lungs as the windows to the mansion shattered. Bullets chopped into the walls repeatedly. The old school Cubans ran toward the front of the mansion with Choppers in their hands before they began to shoot back at the enemy. The walls were being picked apart. Smoke clouds of drywall puffed into the sky as more and more bullets flew in our direction.

I laid on top of Perjah, shielding her from the storm. I had to protect her with everything that I was. I vowed to never let her reach harm.

She screamed in my ear, shaking uncontrollably. "My baby, Tristian. He killed my baby!" Her eyes rolled into the back of her head before she fainted.

To Be Continued...
King of New York 3
Coming Soon

Submission Guideline

Submit the first three chapters of your completed manuscript to ldpsubmissions@gmail.com, subject line: Your book's title. The manuscript must be in a .doc file and sent as an attachment. Document should be in Times New Roman, double spaced and in size 12 font. Also, provide your synopsis and full contact information. If sending multiple submissions, they must each be in a separate email.

Have a story but no way to send it electronically? You can still submit to LDP/Ca$h Presents. Send in the first three chapters, written or typed, of your completed manuscript to:

LDP: Submissions Dept
Po Box 870494
Mesquite, Tx 75187

DO NOT send original manuscript. Must be a duplicate.

Provide your synopsis and a cover letter containing your full contact information.

Thanks for considering LDP and Ca$h Presents.

BOW DOWN TO MY GANGSTA

By **Ca$h**

TORN BETWEEN TWO

By **Coffee**

BLOOD STAINS OF A SHOTTA **III**

By **Jamaica**

STEADY MOBBIN II

By **Marcellus Allen**

BLOOD OF A BOSS **V**

By **Askari**

LOYAL TO THE GAME **IV**

By **T.J. & Jelissa**

A DOPEBOY'S PRAYER **II**

By **Eddie "Wolf" Lee**

IF LOVING YOU IS WRONG… **III**

LOVE ME EVEN WHEN IT HURTS

By **Jelissa**

TRUE SAVAGE **V**

By **Chris Green**

BLAST FOR ME **III**

ROTTEN TO THE CORE **III**

By **Ghost**

ADDICTIED TO THE DRAMA **III**

By **Jamila Mathis**

LIPSTICK KILLAH **III**

CRIME OF PASSION **II**

By **Mimi**

WHAT BAD BITCHES DO **III**

KILL ZONE

By **Aryanna**

THE COST OF LOYALTY **II**

By **Kweli**

SHE FELL IN LOVE WITH A REAL ONE **II**

By **Tamara Butler**

LOVE SHOULDN'T HURT **III**

RENEGADE BOYS **II**

By **Meesha**

CORRUPTED BY A GANGSTA **III**

By **Destiny Skai**

A GANGSTER'S CODE III

By **J-Blunt**

KING OF NEW YORK III

By **T.J. Edwards**

CUM FOR ME **IV**

By **Ca$h & Company**

GORILLAS IN THE BAY

De'Kari

THE STREETS ARE CALLING

Duquie Wilson

<u>**Available Now**</u>

RESTRAINING ORDER **I & II**

By **CA$H & Coffee**

LOVE KNOWS NO BOUNDARIES **I II & III**

By **Coffee**

RAISED AS A GOON I, II, III & IV

BRED BY THE SLUMS I, II, III

BLAST FOR ME I & II

ROTTEN TO THE CORE I II

By **Ghost**

LAY IT DOWN **I & II**

LAST OF A DYING BREED

BLOOD STAINS OF A SHOTTA I & II

By **Jamaica**

LOYAL TO THE GAME

LOYAL TO THE GAME II

LOYAL TO THE GAME III

By **TJ & Jelissa**

BLOODY COMMAS I & II

SKI MASK CARTEL I II & III

KING OF NEW YORK I II

By **T.J. Edwards**

IF LOVING HIM IS WRONG…I & II

By **Jelissa**

WHEN THE STREETS CLAP BACK I & II III

By **Jibril Williams**

A DISTINGUISHED THUG STOLE MY HEART I II & III

LOVE SHOULDN'T HURT I II

RENEGADE BOYS

By **Meesha**

A GANGSTER'S CODE I & II

By **J-Blunt**

PUSH IT TO THE LIMIT

By **Bre' Hayes**

BLOOD OF A BOSS **I, II, III & IV**

By **Askari**

THE STREETS BLEED MURDER **I, II & III**

THE HEART OF A GANGSTA I II& III

By **Jerry Jackson**

CUM FOR ME

CUM FOR ME 2

CUM FOR ME 3

An **LDP Erotica Collaboration**

BRIDE OF A HUSTLA **I II & II**

THE FETTI GIRLS **I, II& III**

CORRUPTED BY A GANGSTA I & II

By **Destiny Skai**

WHEN A GOOD GIRL GOES BAD

By **Adrienne**

A GANGSTER'S REVENGE **I II III & IV**

THE BOSS MAN'S DAUGHTERS

THE BOSS MAN'S DAUGHTERS II

THE BOSSMAN'S DAUGHTERS III

THE BOSSMAN'S DAUGHTERS IV

THE BOSS MAN'S DAUGHTERS **V**

A SAVAGE LOVE **I & II**

BAE BELONGS TO ME

A HUSTLER'S DECEIT I, II

WHAT BAD BITCHES DO I, II

By **Aryanna**

A KINGPIN'S AMBITON

A KINGPIN'S AMBITION **II**

I MURDER FOR THE DOUGH

By **Ambitious**

TRUE SAVAGE

TRUE SAVAGE II

TRUE SAVAGE **III**

TRUE SAVAGE **IV**

By **Chris Green**

A DOPEBOY'S PRAYER

By **Eddie "Wolf" Lee**

THE KING CARTEL **I, II & III**

By **Frank Gresham**

THESE NIGGAS AIN'T LOYAL **I, II & III**

By **Nikki Tee**

GANGSTA SHYT **I II &III**

By **CATO**

THE ULTIMATE BETRAYAL

By **Phoenix**

BOSS'N UP **I , II & III**

By **Royal Nicole**

I LOVE YOU TO DEATH

By **Destiny J**
I RIDE FOR MY HITTA
I STILL RIDE FOR MY HITTA
By **Misty Holt**
LOVE & CHASIN' PAPER
By **Qay Crockett**
TO DIE IN VAIN
By **ASAD**
BROOKLYN HUSTLAZ
By **Boogsy Morina**
BROOKLYN ON LOCK I & II
By **Sonovia**
GANGSTA CITY
By **Teddy Duke**
A DRUG KING AND HIS DIAMOND I & II III
A DOPEMAN'S RICHES
By Nicole Goosby
TRAPHOUSE KING **I II & III**
By **Hood Rich**
LIPSTICK KILLAH **I, II**
CRIME OF PASSION
By **Mimi**
STEADY MOBBN'
By **Marcellus Allen**
WHO SHOT YA **I, II**
Renta

BOOKS BY LDP'S CEO, CA$H

TRUST IN NO MAN

TRUST IN NO MAN 2

TRUST IN NO MAN 3

BONDED BY BLOOD

SHORTY GOT A THUG

THUGS CRY

THUGS CRY 2

THUGS CRY 3

TRUST NO BITCH

TRUST NO BITCH 2

TRUST NO BITCH 3

TIL MY CASKET DROPS

RESTRAINING ORDER

RESTRAINING ORDER 2

IN LOVE WITH A CONVICT

Coming Soon

BONDED BY BLOOD 2

BOW DOWN TO MY GANGSTA

T.J. Edwards

CPSIA information can be obtained
at www.ICGtesting.com
Printed in the USA
LVHW020215160520
655579LV00006B/681